USA TODAY BESTSELLING AUTHOR
SKYE MACKINNON

BOOK FOUR

DAUGHTER OF WINTER

WINTER GODDESS

PERYTON PRESS

skyemackinnon.com

Cover by MoorBooks

Edited by By Clint Watts

Published by Peryton Press

skyemackinnon.com

Cover by MiblArt.

Formatting by Gina Wynn.

Published by Peryton Press.

Contents

To my readers.
Thank you for following Wyn's journey and giving a new
author a chance.
You rock!

What Happened Before

After the loss of her mother and Chesca, Wyn is grieving and is trying to drown her sorrow by taking sparklies. Of course, drugs are no solution and she eventually needs to face her grief. In the process, she kind of manages to kill herself and ends up in the Library of Lives again, where she discovers that her father is still alive.

To save Wyn (and prevent the Palace from collapsing), Beira expends all her magical energy and ends up bedridden and sickly. This means Wyn now has to step into her mother's shoes and rule the Realm. In between her Royal duties, she takes fighting lessons with Thor and has some fun sex with her Guardians (chapter 5, if you want some steaminess).

It turns out that Ada and her men have disappeared together with the dragon shifter who poisoned Wyn. In another unexpected development, the Spring Goddess Flora turns up and becomes Wyn's ally in return for protection from Angus.

A fake Crispin (a clone created by the Morrigan) invades the Palace and almost manages to kill Wyn, but gets stopped in time and ends up in the dungeons, where Arc interrogates him. The prisoner tells them about Castle Tioram, a place in Scotland where the Morrigan has created a Gate that leads to the Demon Realm. Assuming that Wyn's Father is being held there, Frost, Storm and Arc head to Tioram.

When they're in danger, Wyn suddenly finds herself merge with her magic and becomes what she was always meant to be: a Goddess. She manages to help her Guardians and free her father, but now new challenges are up ahead...

The People of the Realm

Family

Wyn, demi-goddess and heroine of this series
Her Guardians: Storm, Frost, Arc and Crispin
Beira, the Queen of Winter and Wyn's mother
James, Wyn's adoptive father
Rose, Wyn's adoptive mother (deceased)

The Council

Gwain, Master of Arms
Ada, Gwain's second-in-command
Tamara, Mistress of the Household (and spy mistress)
Algonquin, Librarian
Zephyr, Master of the Wings
Theodore, Healer
Magnus, former Treasurer
Anthony, the new Treasurer

The People of the Realm

Friends

Blaze, unicorn extraordinaire
Chesca, demoness (deceased)
Aodh, Chesca's lover (deceased)
Flora, Goddess of Spring
Thor, God of Thunder
Lucifer, who's not actually the devil, just a very cheeky God

Enemies

Angus, Summer King
Bridget, his wife
Morrigan, Goddess of Death
Demons... well, they're evil

Prologue

Being a Goddess isn't all it's made out to be. The worst thing isn't the urge to randomly teleport to faraway places, or stopping people from prostrating before me in the street. No, it's the fact that I can no longer see my men as I used to.

My vision has changed; my eyes are no longer human. I see magic, everywhere, in everyone, but it hides their features, makes it impossible to see their bodies. All I see is their magic, their emotions, their souls. I call it their aura, although I'm sure there's a more technical term for it.

It's not the same though. I'd much rather get a glimpse of their faces again. Crispin's cheeky smile, Frost's grin, Arc's mocking eyebrows, even Storm's broody frown. They're hidden from me, despite all my magic. It tears me apart to not be able to watch their expressions as they talk.

They shine and sparkle, their silhouettes bright, so it's not as if I'm blind, but the detail is washed away by the colour of magic. I don't want to see all their innermost secrets. It's not good for our relationship. I wonder if they're scared of me, the new Wyn. Goddess Wynter, they call me, the new Winter Goddess.

I'd give up all my new powers gladly if I could only see their smiles again.

Chapter One

I study the book from the Library of Lives. It appeared on my desk the day I became a deity. No wonder it didn't turn up before then; it probably mentions that I'm not an ordinary demigoddess. No, I'm a Goddess now. Yay me.

I know that I only need to open it for the knowledge inside to seep into my mind. I discovered that new skill yesterday when I randomly opened one of the books lying on my mother's desk. I now know everything about the herbs in her Realm despite never having read a single page in the book. It's scary to know that if I wanted, I could walk through the Royal Library and learn everything in its books within a day. I don't think that would be wise, though. Already, hand-drawn images of herbs keep popping up in my mind at random moments, and that was only a single book. I think my head would explode if I did this with more than a few books.

But the tome in front of me is different. It's about demigods and I know that I'm mentioned in there. Back during my first visit to the Library of Lives, the clerk looked me up in it. It feels like a very long time ago. My first death experience. The guide to Immortality. The fight against a being pretending to be my mother.

It's strange, back then I was so desperate to find out more about demigods, and now I no longer need to. Unless all demigods turn into Gods at some point. No, I doubt that, someone would have warned me. Everyone was just as surprised when I turned into my new me just like I was. I never thought this much power could run through my body without killing me. My magic has grown from a cat into a lion and its cave is barely large enough to keep it contained. Wherever I go, magic happens. Lights start flickering, tiny ice flowers grow on windows, something explodes. Yes, there's been a lot of exploding. Luckily, nobody's got hurt... yet. I have no idea what to do with all the power I now have access to. It's more than double the magic I had before, and then some. I could level the entire Palace if I wanted to. Maybe even the surrounding villages as well. I'm powerful now, and that scares me. Not that I'm going to tell others that. Especially not my Guardians. I want to be the normal, old Wyn when I'm around them, not the Goddess whose head is full of knowledge and new desires.

Someone knocks on the door and I open it with a single thought. I don't even have to think about *how* I use my magic, I just focus on the intended result and it happens. It makes it easier, but also more uncontrollable. What if I put too much energy into the motion and the door was ripped out of its hinges? I could injure someone. That's my greatest fear right now. Hurting others with my new powers.

Before she even says something, I know that it's Tamara. Yet another one of those useful Goddess gifts.

"My Princess, I would like to talk about the coronation again."

I turn around and glare at her.

"No."

Tamara is old, her white hair framing a wrinkled face, but there's a strength in her that rivals that of the generals. She's more important than all of those, too, being the spy mistress that she secretly is.

"It's your mother's wish. Do you really want to go against that?"

"Yes. It's not right."

Mara sighs. We've had this discussion before, and I don't think we'll reach an agreement today either.

"Wyn, she needs you to step up and take her place. There will be war soon and she can't lead our people in her current condition."

"I can lead them as Princess," I say with as much authority as I can muster to prove my point. "I don't need to be Queen for that."

"I've told you, there are powers that come with being crowned Queen. Powers to lead, to heal, to give the people confidence. You need to inspire them, and while at the moment they're all fascinated by your ascension to Godhood, that won't last forever. Certainly not in battle when they're facing an enemy's sword."

I shake my head. "My mother will heal. Once she's back to how she was before, what happens then? Will there be two Queens?"

Tamara's fierce eyes soften a little. "You know she won't recover. Not until the Summer King has been pushed back, but by then it might be too late. We need you now, Wyn. We need you as our Queen."

"No. I can't."

I sink back into my large leather chair. It's an impossible situation. My mother won't get better until the war is over, but to win the war, we need a Queen. I can't do it, though, I just can't. It feels like betrayal and treason against my mother, even though she's the one who made the suggestion.

Demand, actually. My mother didn't ask me to take her role. She told me to do it.

"How's my father?" I ask, hoping to change the topic. I don't doubt for a second that Tamara will try again, but hopefully, I'm getting a short reprieve.

"He's asked to see you." She turns to leave. "Maybe you'll listen to him."

As soon as she's out of the door, I make my magic close the door. I may intentionally have put too much force into it, so it slams shut with a bang. Oops. Well, nobody will dare tell me off. Even if I'm not the Queen, people have started treating me as such, even the Council members. It's annoying.

I sign two more papers that someone, probably Mara, put in my in-tray, then leave my office to head to the Royal Quarters. Two days ago, my father was released from the hospital wing to recover in a more comfortable environment. Physically, he's mostly healed, but not so much mentally. Both my mum's death and his imprisonment have left their traces on him. He's not the man I remember. He was always an emotional person, but now he's on the verge of tears pretty much whenever I see him. I envy him that he's allowed to show his emotions so openly. I have to keep up the facade so that my subjects don't see how I'm feeling inside. How broken I am.

Two guards are standing in front of the doors leading to my father's new rooms. They bow deeply when they see me approach and open the double doors for me. At least they're not calling me 'Queen' like some of the other guards recently. I had to threaten them with demotion if they ever do that again. It's treason.

My father is still in bed, his form only a small bulge under the sheets. He's lost a lot of weight during his imprisonment, and despite the cooks making all his favourite dishes, he's not eating much. I think he's lost the will to continue going on like before. He doesn't look after himself either; his beard is a shaggy mess, so different from the clean-shaven father I was used to. I'll tell one of the barbers to visit him. Maybe it's just because he's been too weak to shave himself.

"Dad, how are you?"

He's awake, staring at the ceiling. My heart begins to ache at the pitiful sight of him. This isn't supposed to be like that. He was always a role model for me, even despite his ditziness.

"Dad?" I ask again, sitting down on the edge of the bed.

He doesn't react, just keeps staring up. I take a quick look myself to see if there's anything special up there, but no, it's just a normal, boring ceiling. There are not even any of the floating lights there.

"Is there anything I can do for you?" I ask softly, taking his hands in mine. Finally, he seems to realise that I'm here.

"Wyn?"

"Yup, as I live and breathe."

21

He doesn't smile, at least his aura doesn't show any trace of humour.

"Was it a nightmare?" he asks slowly.

My heart hurts even more at the false hope in his voice. "No, dad, it wasn't. She's gone."

"She was so brave," he mutters. "So very brave. Just like you."

I cringe. "I'm not brave. If I was, I'd already be in the Morrigan's castle, making her pay for what she did. But no, I ran like a coward."

He sits up a little and I help him by pushing a pillow under his back.

"You had people to protect. Sometimes, not staying to fight is braver than taking up arms."

I stare at him. "When did you become a philosopher?"

He grimaces. "Always been one. I've just never had a chance to talk about battles and courage before. I wish I didn't have to now."

"Me too," I sigh. "The world has become very strange. Some days, I just want to go back to Earth and live my human life again."

"No," he says, his voice a little stronger now. "You belong here. This is your world, Wyn. Our life has never been enough for you. You're destined to be something bigger than us, and I think you know that. Look at yourself, look at how they treat you. You're special, darling."

I shake my head. "I wish I wasn't."

"We all want to be someone we're not," he says, his voice sounding as if he's smiling. I wish I could see his face properly.

"I don't want to be a widower. I don't want to be a victim of the Morrigan. But you know what? I'm proud to be the father of a Goddess."

His aura is sparkling with pride. I want to tell him that I'm not a proper Goddess, that I'm nothing to be proud of, but I don't want to extinguish that spark.

"If you're feeling up to it, I can introduce you to the Court," I say instead, taking advantage of him being more energetic than he usually is. "They're all very curious about the human who raised me."

"Oh no, I don't think that's something for me. Your mother would have loved it, I'm sure, but I'd rather stay here, if you don't mind. I'm not made for crowds."

I smile. "Yes, I'd rather stay here too, if I'm honest. Part of the job though." I sigh. "I should get back. There's a Council meeting later on that I need to prepare for. I think it's going to be a long one."

"I'm not envying you. Although that Tamara woman seems very capable."

"Mara has been here?"

"Oh yes, she wanted to know about the prison I was kept in. She was very gentle about it."

Somehow, I can't imagine Tamara being very gentle, but if he thinks so, that's good. Glad I have one thing less on my list. I'd waited until now to ask him questions about what happened to him. Storm gave me a full report after we returned to the Palace, and he got a good enough overview of the Morrigan's hideout.

I can't believe it's only been a week since we returned from there. So much has happened, and yet, not as much as there could have been. My personal life has changed, my whole being has, but the political situation hasn't. We've not heard anything from the Morrigan since we broke my father out of her dungeons. She's no longer in that place, and just in case she returns, we have spies monitoring the Gate.

Angus has stopped moving his troops, but they're close to the borders. It's as if everyone is holding their breath, waiting for the inevitable moment when the big battle begins. For now, I hope we can prolong this time of peace. Well, maybe not peace. The absence of outright war.

I say goodbye to my father and tell one of the guards at the door to call for the barber. Let's see if my dad will get the hint.

I return to my office, feeling a little better. As traumatised as my dad seemed when I got in to visit him, he did become more like his old self towards the end. That's progress and it gives me hope.

I close my office door behind me and lean against it, taking a deep breath. Back to being the Heiress.

"Tough day?"

I jump and ready my magic, before I notice that Frost is sitting on my chair, his legs propped up on the desk.

"What are you doing here?" I push my magic back, despite her struggling.

"Coming to see how you are." There's humour in his voice and I'm sure he's smiling. I wish I could see it.

"You look sad," he says softly and gets up from his chair.

"Not used to all the changes," I mutter and sink into his hug. "The eye thing is getting to me."

He hugs me tight. "We'll find a solution. Your mother can see normally, so I'm sure there's a way. Besides, why ever would you want to look at us? Crispin's the only pretty one."

I laugh. "Are you trying to make me say that you're all rather handsome looking?"

"Got me. Now, say it."

Instead, I kiss him. Luckily, my body is well acquainted with Frost's and knows exactly where his lips are waiting for me. I don't need my vision for that.

He opens his lips and lets me in. I kiss him hard, possessively, showing him that he's mine and that I won't let him go. I almost lost him last week, and I'm not intending for this to ever happen again. Death isn't allowed to come between us. Not between me and Frost, and not between any of the other guys either. Dying isn't allowed.

Our tongues dance and he shifts his hands on my back, sliding them lower until they reach the waistband of my trousers. I'm refusing to wear dresses at the moment. It doesn't feel right to be wearing pretty clothes while half the country is readying for war. At least that's my excuse.

He slips a hand under the fabric and runs it over my naked skin.

"I want you," he mutters, breathing hard.

I don't bother replying. I'm sure he knows how much I want him from my hard nipples pressing against his chest, and my fumbling fingers on his belt. Why does he always need to wear a belt? It's making things difficult.

Then I remember that I'm a Goddess now and grin.

"Look what I can do," I whisper and tell my magic to intervene.

"I'm naked," Frost observes a second later. "You too."

"That was the point of it," I chuckle. "Look at the desk."

He turns around and laughs. "You're very efficient."

"Perks of the job." I've lifted all the things that were lying on the desk and deposited them in a corner of the room. I've never had sex on a table before, but it sounds like something that could be quite a lot of fun.

Without warning, Frost picks me up and carries me towards the desk. I wrap my legs around him, already feeling his erection hard against my arse. I don't think we have any need for foreplay today.

He sits me down on the table and bends down to kiss me again. His breath is hot against mine; his fresh seaweed scent caressing my senses. My Frost.

I cling to him, encourage him to push forward and enter me. He doesn't need much encouragement. His cock is hard and I'm ready for him. He glides into me without much resistance and I moan against his kiss. I think my fingernails are leaving red streaks on his back, but he doesn't complain. He starts to increase his rhythm, driving into me faster and faster. My breasts are rubbing against his chest, sending tiny lightning bolts all the way down to my core.

The table groans beneath us, but I send some magic into it to make sure it won't collapse. That would be such a turn-off.

The closer I get to the point of no return, the louder my moans get. Frost is breathing hard, his lips meeting mine whenever he pushes into me, then leave again a second later. It's a cat and mouse game that's driving me crazy. I could use magic to keep him close, but I don't think he'd appreciate that.

I know he's probably looking at me, but I can't tell it from the bright silhouette I see him as. Golden light is shimmering all around him, and suddenly turns into thousands of tiny sparks when he comes in me. I need a second longer, one more push of his cock into my core, then I come apart, wrapping my arms around his neck to steady myself. Shivers rack through me - and something explodes.

"Wyn, get your magic under control," Frost warns, but it's too late. Sparks are flying, rainbow clouds are erupting all over the room, and the smell of burning wood reaches my nose.

"What did I do?" It's hard to focus, my mind is still shattered into very happy pieces.

"Ehm... bookshelf... let me."

He steps back and I can see him gather his water magic, the azure blue of it contrasting on his usual gold. It's strange seeing someone else do magic. He sends out his magical energy towards the bookshelf, like a net of blue fibres, and then once they reach the shelf, he sends a spark there that makes them erupt into water. That's probably not how it actually works, but it's what my new senses tell me.

"Did I burn any books?"

I'm refusing to turn around and look at the damage. Can't I have normal sex just once? There always seem to be explosions, burns, or someone interrupting us. At least this time we both got to climax before the inevitable happened.

"Just one."

"Tell me... oh. I think I know which one."

I make the remains of the book fly towards me and take them into my hands. Fragments of knowledge jump into my mind, jumbled and broken. The book isn't salvageable, that's for sure.

"Frost?" I ask carefully. "You know how the Library of Lives states that non-return of a book results in decapitation? What do you think the punishment is for burning one of their books?"

His groan is answer enough. There's going to be one very angry librarian somewhere.

Chapter Two

Storm is the only Council member absent. He's at the Southern border today, inspecting our troops. I teleported him there this morning and will collect him again tonight. It's a handy trick, saving him a long flight. Right now, speed counts. We don't know when and where our enemies will attack - but it's safe to say that it won't be long.

I'm about to start the session when the door bursts open.

"Your Majesty, there's a visitor."

I frown at the servant. "We're having a Council meeting now. I'm sure this visitor can wait."

The servant cringes at my words but remains where he is.

"My lady... it's not a normal visitor. He's not even... I'm sorry, Your Majesty, but he's a unicorn!"

I begin to laugh. "Is his name Blaze?"

He nods. "Yes, he introduced himself as Lord Blaze. I'm not sure if he's really a lord, or if that's how unicorns usually speak..."

"You may leave now," Gwain interrupts the servant.

"I'm going to see to Blaze," I announce, already halfway out of the room. "If the unicorn comes here to the Palace, it has to be important."

"We'll discuss the not so important things while you're gone," Tamara promises. That gives me a reason to take my time. The more of the Council session I can miss, the better. I don't get why we have to discuss all the small matters while war is at our doorstep. Who cares about land disputes and food taxes right now. Well, some Council members do, obviously. And sadly, I have to keep them happy so that they support me in the important matters. Like the upcoming battles. Sigh. Life as royalty really isn't all it's made out to be.

I hurry to the main antechamber, where I assume Blaze is. Wait, I don't need to assume. I extend my magic and ask it to find the unicorn - and I'm glad that I did. Blaze isn't indoors at all, instead, he's waiting in a courtyard close the Palace entrance. Maybe he doesn't want to be around too many humans.

I change direction and take one of the slides to get down to ground level quicker. The stair slides are still my favourite thing about this Palace. I tell it "Queen" and sit on the top stair. A second later, the stairs turn into a smooth slide and I'm whisked away at breakneck speed. I love how they named the highest speed setting Queen. Now that I'm in my mother's role, I totally understand. I always need to be fast when I want to get there.

Oh. I could have teleported. Silly me. Did I mention I'm still getting used to my new powers?

Well, now it's not really worth the use of magic. I turn around two corners and enter the courtyard through a white wooden door, delicately carved with vines and flowers.

Blaze is awkwardly standing in the centre of the square, nudging a weird looking flower with his horn. He must be bored.

The unicorn is fascinating to look at. He's sparkling throughout, not just on the outside. His aura is covered in rainbow sparkles, not unlike the rainbow mist in his cave. His horn though is the most extraordinary thing about his appearance. It's where all of his magic seems to be concentrated, swirling and writhing in the confined space. His magic is bright silver, almost too bright, and a lot more powerful than I had imagined.

"Blaze," I say loudly and he turns around. "What a pleasure to see you again." I remember how I last saw him, singed and scared of me, and add, "I apologise for what happened last time. I wasn't quite myself."

He bows his head. "I know, don't worry about it. I didn't leave because of you. I was called away."

"Is that so?" I take a seat on one of the benches. It's freezing cold and I funnel some magic into the metal to make it nice and cosy. Before, I would have had to do a lot of complicated thinking to achieve this, now, I just think 'get warm' and it happens. I would have never had to take lessons with my guys if magic had been this easy from the beginning. At the same time, I'm glad that I have acquired a detailed knowledge of how magic works. If I ever lose these new powers, I won't have to start back at zero.

"I have news from a friend of yours," Blaze begins. "But first, I've heard Queen Beira is unwell?"

I nod and sigh. "Yes, she's been ill for some time. I've taken over her duties until she recovers."

"Will she recover?" Blaze asks, his voice a little sharper than I'm used to. I look at him in surprise.

"Yes. Once Angus has been defeated."

"Are you sure?" The unicorn sounds as if he doesn't believe me in the slightest.

I sigh again. "Yes. Now, what's that message? What friend?"

"The pretty Guardian who went to the dragons. Ada."

"Wait, you know where Ada is?" I almost jump up from the bench in surprise, but just about manage to control myself. Behaving like that wouldn't be very Queen-like. Princess-like, I mean. I'm not the Queen.

"Yes, I do. She called me to her, even though she didn't know that she was doing it. She and her Guardians have travelled far and have had quite a few adventures. I'm not sure I believe all she's told me, but who knows, maybe it's true. Anyway, she's followed that dragon to his Realm."

"The Dragon Realm?" I interrupt. "We thought that they support the Morrigan. They've not replied to any of our messages, and their ambassador has disappeared."

"They didn't support her, not willingly at least. She had a hold on them, but not any longer. Ada says the dragons will support you, but they want to meet you in person first. They want to decide whether you're strong enough to lead them into battle." He chuckles. "They're almost as proud as unicorns."

I let his words run through my mind again. Dragons. Ada. The prisoner. I'd almost forgotten about her and the man she'd freed from our dungeons. There had been a lot more important things to deal with, and we didn't have the resources to invest in searching for them. Now, I'm quite glad we didn't. It seems she's managed to achieve quite a feat by herself.

"Where do they want to meet?" I ask Blaze. "Are they coming here?"

He shakes his large head. "No, they aren't trusting enough for that. When you find out what happened to them, you'll understand. They want you to come to the Dragon Realm, and soon. I'd recommend tomorrow."

I gape at him. "Tomorrow? Do you know how full my schedule is? I can't just disappear on a merry trip to dragon land."

He whinnies. "You're a Goddess now, Wyn. You can do whatever you want."

"How do you know I'm a Goddess?"

"You smell different. I bet the sparklies wouldn't have as big of an effect on you now as they used to. Want to try?"

I shudder at the memory of the first time I took his sparklies. I'd turned into a hormonal, lovesick weirdo. Then, I got addicted. No, I don't ever want to get near that stuff again.

"Are you trying to provoke me?" I ask the unicorn and he snickers.

"Maybe. It's fun. Now, do you think I could get some food? It's been a long ride here."

I smile. "What would you like? I don't think I know what unicorns eat, to be honest."

"Magic. We eat magic. You should know that by now."

"How does that work?" I ask. I didn't have a clue. When we had our very first picnic in his cave, he didn't eat with us, and on my visits after, I never saw him eat either. But magic? Is he eating *my* magic?

"It's like grazing. There's magic all around, it just needs to be lapped up. And in a Palace like this, the magic is almost overflowing. I can taste it. You just need to show me to a place where there's lots of magic being used, and I'll be happy."

I think for a moment. "One of the training courtyards is probably the best. There should be lots of magic there."

I lead Blaze through the Palace, probably earning a lot of curious glances. For once, I'm glad I can't see people's faces. I'm not sure many of them have ever seen a unicorn before. My Guardians said that Blaze was the only one they ever met, and they've travelled a lot more than most Palace inhabitants.

When we enter the closest training courtyard, there are a few Guardians running around, shooting magic at each other. Most of the fighting lessons has been postponed to make way for war preparations, but a few are still taking place for the least experienced Guardians. My mother stopped creating new ones long ago, but some of the other strong Gods and Goddesses still create Guardians occasionally, many of which end up here at the Palace to serve, entertain and probably spy on us.

When the first one sees us, he shrieks and takes his eyes off his opponent. I swipe away the ball of fire that would have hit him and shoo them away. They bow and run. Am I really this scary?

"You could have let them stay," Blaze complains. "Their magic tasted good."

I shrug. "Too late. Is there enough food for you here?"

He lowers his head to the ground and his horn begins to sparkle even more. With my new senses, I can see how magic is being pulled from the environment into his horn. Fascinating.

"Will this take long?" I ask him, watching as more and more magic is slowly dragged towards Blaze.

"Yummy," the unicorn says, sounding as if he's chewing something. "Maybe an hour, maybe two. There's a lot of magic here. Such a waste. I should come more often."

An hour? Seriously? Then again, our big feasts take a lot longer than that, so I guess I should cut him some slack.

"I'll leave you alone to enjoy your meal. Just tell a guard when you're ready and I'll come back."

Blaze doesn't answer, too occupied with munching magic.

I smile and leave him to it, heading back to the Council chambers.

I can hear the noise from far away. It must be a lively session. The Council has been less divided since I disposed of Magnus, the treasurer, and replaced him with Anthony, but there's always a lot of debate. All the members of the Council are used to being experts in their particular field and don't usually get a lot of criticism.

I sigh and enter the room without warning. They all fall silent. Good.

I head to my almost-throne at the top of the table and sit, staring them down.

"What's the problem?" I ask after letting them wait for a few seconds, turning to Tamara.

"While you were gone, we got news. The clone is dead."

"The fake Crispin?"

After Arc interrogated him and we found out where the Morrigan was hiding, I'd not given any thought to him. He was to stay in the dungeons forever. I couldn't kill him, not when he looked so much like Crispin. Arc told me that he was nothing like Crispin inside, but no, executing him wasn't an option. So I'd told the guards that he was to remain in prison indefinitely.

"Yes," Tamara responds. "He was found dead an hour ago. They've not been able to establish how he died yet, but there are no obvious wounds."

"He was stripped and searched when he was put in his cell, so it can't have been poison," healer Theodore says confidently.

I shake my head. "It could have been if someone gave it to him. Or maybe the Morrigan can kill her creations from a distance?"

Theodore nods grudgingly. "I will examine him after this meeting."

"I will come with you," I announce. His aura turns darker; I bet his expression sours as well. He doesn't like me, but I don't know why. Not that I'm a big fan of him either.

"Now, what else is there that we need to discuss?"

Tamara looks at the papers in front of her. "We now have letters from several Gods where they confirm in writing that they're going to support us. Most of them have promised a relatively small number of warriors, probably wanting to see how you'll respond. I recommend asking for at least double of what they propose."

I nod. "Do it."

"The Spring Realm is fortified and our officers are helping train their soldiers. No reports of enemies have been made, but I'm sure Angus is monitoring the situation."

"What do we know of Angus's movements?" I ask, anxious to skip the small bits and move on to the bigger, important news.

"Not much. He's kept his armies in the same position for weeks now. We still regularly intercept spies and scouts within our Realm, but no more than usual. It's like he's waiting for something."

"No doubt the Morrigan," I mutter. "She's still not been seen?"

Tamara shakes her head. "No, and neither have any demons. None at all, which is extremely suspicious."

"Not a single demon?" I ask, knowing how strange that is. There are always demons causing mayhem, whether it's on Earth or in other Realms. Rarely in this one as our Gates are well guarded, but there have been some who've come through, probably by accident. They usually get killed on sight.

"Not a single one," Gwain confirms. "It's making my men anxious. The absence of demons is worse than having them where we can see them."

Yes, I get where he's coming from. Most demons aren't very clever, but now that the Morrigan has taken over their Realm, we have to assume that she's in complete control, which makes everything to do with demons very suspicious.

"Is there any chance we can get some scouts into the Demon Realm?" I ask them, but Gwain immediately shakes his head.

"The Castle Tioram Gate has closed as if it had never been there in the first place. I've never seen anything like it. The Gate looks dead, like it'll never work again. Of course, we still have a few people stationed there to monitor the situation. The problem is, sending my scouts via our Gates into the demon Realms would be a suicide mission. I'm not willing to risk that."

I sigh. "I wish we still had Aodh and Chesca. They rehabilitated several demons that might be willing to help us, but without them, we have no chance of finding them."

"And remember what happened last time you trusted a rehabilitated demon," Tamara mutters, reminding me of the day my parents got kidnapped. True, I don't think I could ever trust a demon again.

"So basically, we have no idea what's happening with the demons, or the Morrigan, and in some ways, Angus?" I summarise, a sinking feeling spreading in my stomach.

Gwain sighs deeply. "That's correct, Your Majesty. For now, it seems all we can do is wait. Alternatively, we could be the ones to start the battle, but I don't recommend it without having more intel on the Morrigan's plans."

"I agree. I have news myself, though," I announce and I feel all their gazes on me, despite not being able to see their eyes.

Maybe I'm just imagining it, or maybe it's my strange new magic sense. "The dragons have been in touch."

I smile at their reactions.

"The dragons, Your Highness?" Algonquin asks, his aura swirling with excitement.

"Yes, the dragons." I turn to Gwain. "It seems your deputy hasn't abandoned us."

"Ada?" His voice is full of wonder and surprise. "She's contacted you?"

My smile widens. "Via a unicorn, yes. I don't know the details, but it seems that she's travelled to the Dragon Realm and somehow convinced them to help us. Having the dragons on board will be invaluable." I don't say that I've never seen a shifted dragon, so I have no idea how good they are in a fight. For all I know, they could be tiny, but I'm not letting that dampen my enthusiasm. "Blaze - that's the unicorn - says they want to meet me first to decide whether we're worthy of their support."

"That could be a trap," Gwain says immediately. "How much do you trust that unicorn?"

A grey swirl floats through his aura. Is that doubt? It's going to take me a long time to figure out what all the colours mean. This might be more accurate than reading facial expressions, but a lot more confusing.

I think back to how I met Blaze, how he kept me supplied with sparklies. He was my drug dealer, so to speak, but somehow, I trust him completely. His aura is pure and there's no deceit in there, despite all his snarkiness.

"He's trustworthy," I say firmly. "If he says he's met Ada, he really has. And from what I know about Ada, she's as loyal as they come."

Gwain nods. "I should have never doubted her," he mutters sadly. "She's always been a great soldier, and a friend."

"You weren't the only one," Tamara says soothingly. "I doubted her myself after she disappeared. I think we'll have to apologise when she returns."

Anthony clears his throat, surprising me. He's an excellent treasurer, but he rarely speaks up in Council meetings. "Even if Ada and the unicorn are to be trusted, who says the dragons aren't lying to them? They could be using them to get you to their Realm."

"True," I concede. "But it's too great an opportunity to miss out on. I'll travel there and I will take my four Guardians with me. Not that I can't protect myself, but it's good to have the extra eyes and ears."

I can feel the advisors' dissent and worry, but I've made my decision.

Tomorrow, I'm going to meet some dragons.

Chapter Three

It's just like old times. My men and I, on a quest to find allies and defeat demons. Except that I'm now a Goddess and can teleport us, saving the need for portable thrones, Gates and flying. My advisors have told me that it's polite to teleport to a Gate in the Dragon Realm rather than into one of their settlements. Not that I have any idea about their Realm. It's shrouded in mystery and few people have ever seen it. Dragons are reclusive by nature and prefer to send their ambassadors to other Realms rather than allowing envoys into their lands.

Algonquin gave me a book about dragons and I touched it, so now I have the entire contents of it swirling in my brain. They're not quite settled yet and a light headache is pulsating behind my temples.

I laugh softly.

"What?" Frost asks immediately.

"I have a book in my head." I giggle at the absurdness of the situation. "I touched a book and now it's in my head. Goddess powers are weird."

He laughs as well. "Are you saying you weren't weird before?"

I put my hands on my hips in mock outrage. "I've never been weird. I'm normal, it's just that the rest of the world isn't."

"Ooookay then," Crispin says from behind, arriving with the other two. "Let's just pretend I didn't hear that, otherwise I'll take that as an insult. I'm not weird. I'm Crispin."

"Ye say that as if that's a special category," Arc mutters.

"Well, it is," Crispin replies cheerfully. "There's Wyns, Crispins and weirdos."

Storm sighs. "Could we all be a bit more serious? We're about to journey into an unfamiliar Realm and we have no idea what awaits us there. Maybe we should be preparing for that rather than behaving like children."

"Are you accusing the Princess of this Realm to be childish?" I protest with a grin. "I could have you punished for treason."

Storm bends down and whispers in my ear, "If anyone's going to do punishing, it will be me."

I shiver at the sweet promise in his tone. I love his dominant side, even though he's not had much of a chance to show it recently. Once all this is over, I'm going to lock my guys into a bedroom and not let them out until we've spent some quality time with each other. Naked, preferably.

I take a deep breath. I'd better behave like Royalty from now on. According to the book in my head, dragons are fiercely proud and keen on following tradition. Even though I have no idea about what their traditions are exactly, I'm sure there's going to be a lot of pomp and ceremony. That's why I'm wearing a dress. Urgh. It seemed more appropriate than the jeans and blouse I was wearing to the Council meeting. People here have kind of got used to my ungodly dress sense, but the dragons haven't met me yet. Dress it is.

"Ready?" I ask the guys and I can feel their ascent through our bond. "Hold onto me."

Arc hugs me from behind, his broad chest tight against my back. I wish I had time to enjoy his touch, but that's wishful thinking. The others take hold of my arms and off we go.

There's no way to describe teleporting. It's instinctive, a raw power that is far too slippery to put into words. I think of the place I want to go, and then we're there, even though it's a lot more complicated than that.

It takes less time than the blink of an eye.

Warmth assaults my senses, the kind of heat that presses against your body and makes you want to rip off your clothes. I'm glad I predicted this and am wearing one of my lighter dresses. The guys will be sweltering in their armour. I send some cooling air to them, wishing it was me rather than the air that hugs them. Arc has already stepped back, no longer embracing me from behind. Probably because five huge women are staring at us.

They're at least six feet tall each and very, very wide. Not fat, just... wide. Like their shoulders and hips are broader than they should anatomically be. These women certainly aren't human.

Elaborate helmets cover their heads, each of them having differently shaped horns sprouting from the glinting metal. They remind me of Viking helmets, even though I know that the Vikings never actually had horns on theirs. That's just a myth, just like so many legends and stories.

The woman in the centre of the five steps forward. Her bright red hair frames a stern face. A large scar makes its way from her left cheek up to her hairline, giving her an even fiercer look. She could be wearing a summer dress like me and still look like a warrior.

"Princess Wynter?" she asks in a pleasant, but serious voice.

I step forward as well, sensing that my men are taking their positions behind me.

"Yes, thank you for the invitation. Who do I have the pleasure of meeting?"

The woman bows her head. "I am Agierth, Protector of the Sky. These are my sisters Ynade and Torsei," she points to the two women on the left, "as well as Gayghys and Fraedurth."

I know already that I'll have trouble remembering those names. They're not exactly common.

"It's a pleasure to meet you," I reply, not quite sure if there's a protocol I should be following. "I've been told that Ada, my Mistress of Arms, is with you?"

Agierth nods. "She is waiting for you, along with our Royal Ladies. Follow us."

I assumed we were going to walk or fly, but one of the women - Torsei, perhaps - turns around and waves her hands in the air, moving in a complicated circular pattern. I watch in fascination as magic is drawn from the environment and weaved into a thick rope. I've never seen anything like it, although I know that I could easily replicate it, now that I have my Goddess powers. The woman works on the rope until it's about three times as long as herself, then she flings it into the air, binding the two ends together to form a circle. The magic within the ropes crackles and spreads, merging with itself over and over again until the inside of the circle is covered with a thin layer of magic. I've seen this kind of structure before. It's a Gate!

It won't be stable forever, and it's certainly not permanent, but this woman has managed to create a Gate within a few minutes.

"Is that what I think it is?" Storm mutters from behind me so that the women won't hear.

"Yes," I reply just as quietly. "And I know how to replicate it. Imagine how easily we'll be able to transport our forces from A to B without me having to teleport them."

"Already it seems like a good idea coming here," Frost observes. "Even if we don't manage to get them on board, we'll have learned something to aid us in the future."

"Come," Agierth says in a voice that's almost a command. "It won't stay open for long."

Two of her sisters step through the Gate first, then Agierth. The other two are waiting for us to follow.

"Let's do this," I say confidently and walk towards the Gate. Its magic is calling to me, whispering secrets and memories. The woman who made the Gate must have poured more of herself into it than she realised. I try to block it out, but some of her thoughts make their way into my mind nonetheless. I shudder when one particular memory floods my senses. I push it to one side to examine it later.

"What's wrong?" Storm asks as I sway at the intensity of the images.

"Nothing," I mutter and take the final step through the Gate, knowing that my Guardians will be just behind me.

It's a rough ride, not at all like normal Gates. Not that they're always pleasant to travel through, but they don't make me feel like I'm almost ripped apart. When the Gate finally spits me out, I need a moment to steady myself, before I can look at where we've landed.

It's even hotter here than where we first entered the Realm, and I wish I could be in a bikini rather than a dress. How do people here cope with that heat? Maybe if I hadn't grown up in Scotland I'd be more used to warm weather, but right now, I can't change that. I summon some more cool air to surround me and my Guardians, who've just stepped out of the Gate.

"I dinnae like that," Arc announces. "I'm a wee bit queasy."

"Tell me about it," Frost says, his voice quivering. "I think I'm about to throw up."

I make my magic heal his upset stomach with a single thought and then do the same to the others, just in case. I don't want any of them to throw up in the Dragon Palace.

"Wyn, did you do that?" Frost asks in wonder.

I shrug. "It's easy."

Crispin steps to my side. "It's not. It would have taken me at least a minute to do that for all of us, and I'm an experienced healer. Your magic is incredible, Wyn."

I feel a blush rise in my cheeks. I don't feel like I can be proud of my new powers. I didn't do anything to deserve them. I'm grateful to have them, sure, they helped me save Frost and my father, but they don't feel like they're mine yet.

I shrug it off and finally look around properly. We're in a large open space surrounded by red sandstone walls, as tall as some of the largest tower blocks back in Edinburgh. Perched on top of it are dragons. Giant fricking dragons, so much more imposing than any film or painting on Earth could have ever portrayed them. They're too beautiful to be real. One of them has his wings - or maybe her wings? - unfolded, stretching them high into the sky. Red sunlight is shining through the wing's membranes, making them shimmer and sparkle. There are horns on the dragons' heads, just like the horns on the women's helmets. Maybe they're the same shape as when they're shifted? Or... maybe the horns aren't on the helmets, but real, growing on the women's heads?

The five women who greeted us are waiting in front, watching us. I can't see their expressions to know if they're impatient, but their auras aren't giving me any negative vibes.

The large walled expanse we're in leads to enormous brass doors at the top of some steps. The palace must lie beyond those doors.

I'm about to tell the women that we're ready to continue on when something darkens the sky. I look up, expecting a large cloud perhaps that's covering the sun, but no, it's a dragon. It's bigger even than the dragons perched on the walls, and its scales seem smoother somehow, reflecting the sunlight and breaking it into a million specks of light. While the other dragons are mostly red and earth colours, this one is bright blue, with shades of sapphire mixing with lapis lazuli. I wouldn't be surprised if the scales were actually made of gemstones.

The dragon flaps its wings, making enough wind for my hair to fly into my face. Oh yes, did I mention? Becoming a Goddess made my hair grow back. It's a lot longer now than before, reaching almost to my hips, and I keep wanting to cut it, but so far, I've not been able to persuade the hairdresser to do it. Maybe I should get some scissors and do it myself. The length just isn't practical.

It lands in front of us, making the ground tremble. The wings are still extended, showing the muscles and sinews that enable this giant dragon to fly. Two horns grow on either side of its skull, turning several times into delicate spirals. Its snout is large and with its mouth open, I can see big, sharp teeth protruding from its gums. It's beautiful, but also not a being I'd want to mess with. It could swallow me whole before I could fight back with magic.

What's strange though is that I can see it. My new vision allows me to see structures and plants as I did before, but all Gods and Guardians are hidden behind their auras, not letting me see their features. I'd assumed that it would be the same for dragons. Maybe they're too much like animals? Not that I'm complaining, it's amazing to see all the beautiful details of their powerful bodies.

The dragon roars, freezing cold air enveloping us. I instinctively pull some of the hot air from around us and wrap it around the guys and myself. It's such a strange thing to have ice dragons living in this hot climate.

A strange blue mist is gathering around the dragon, the same colour as its scales. It doesn't seem like magic to my new senses, but what else can it be. You can't tell me mist suddenly appears out of nowhere, especially not blue and concentrated only in that one area.

The fog thickens until the dragon is covered in it, hidden by all the blueness.

"Do you think he's shifting?" Arc asks from behind me, but before anyone can answer, we see that he was right. With a gust of wind, the blue mist is blown away, revealing one of the most stunning women I've ever seen. A sleek blue dress hugs her wide hips and ample cleavage, and I'm not surprised that the fabric of the dress is the same colour as the dragon scales were moments ago.

She is just as tall as the women who welcomed us, if not taller. Her horns are delicate spirals, thick where they're surrounded by her lush black hair, and thin and pointy at the ends. They're shimmering with a slight silver hue, just like the horns on the dragon did. Oh my. It's just what I'd thought. The horns aren't on the helmets. The women have horns. Wow. Don't they get in the way? So far we've only seen female dragon shifters. Do men have the same horns? Don't they get in the way of kissing?

Silly Wyn, of course that's the first thing I'm thinking of. Kissing. I should be focussed on the dragon woman now walking towards us.

Her gait is slightly different from how humans and Guardians walk, heavier and more cautious, as if she's used to carrying more bulk around with her. That doesn't make her any less elegant and regal though. She's a woman who shouldn't be messed with, that's for sure.

"Are her eyes blue?" I whisper so only the guys can hear. Her face is shrouded in her magic aura, although it's less intense as with other people. I can almost make out her features, but there's still a lot of guesswork involved.

"Yes, the same blue her scales were," Frost confirms. "She's really quite something."

"Oi, stop ogling her," I admonish him, only half in jest. He's mine, and it's going to stay that way.

"Don't worry, I'm not into horns," he mutters and I can hear the grin in his voice.

Storm clears his throat. "Shut up, that could be interpreted as racist."

"Hornist," Crispin chuckles.

"Shut it," Storm repeats and they all fall quiet, just in time as the dragon woman is now in earshot. If she has normal hearing, that is. Her ears look like they're a fairly standard size.

There's movement behind us and I turn around. The five sisters - if they actually are sisters, maybe that's just a term they use here - have been standing behind us, but now, Agierth strides forward, passes our little group and heads towards the dragon lady. And kisses her. Hard. On the mouth.

Storm clears his throat again. Yup, I'm not sure what I'm seeing either. Is it normal here to kiss like this in public? Agierth's hands are tousling the other woman's hair, who in turn has wrapped her arms around Agierth's waist, her fingers almost touching her bum. It's a very public display of affection.

I'm not quite sure what to do and whether it's even okay to watch them. Maybe they expect everyone to look away? Or do they want us to see?

I've almost got used to seeing half-naked Guardians and Gods in my mother's Palace, but that's just physical affection, a way to satisfy their desires. This here is different. I can see the love the two women have for each other in their auras which have now turned a shade of red. It's the same colour I see when my men are close to me. I always thought my favourite colour was blue, but ever since my vision changed, I've preferred red. The colour of love. How predictable and yet beautiful.

Finally, the two women break apart. I'm feeling a little ignored, if I'm to be honest. I'm the Heiress to the Winter Realm, I've travelled far to get here, and I could be doing war preparations just now. Yes, I want their help, but the way they ignore us is a little over the top.

I step forward to bring some attention to myself. It's working. The woman in the blue dress focusses her attention on me - and her magic. It's spreading through the air around me as if it wants to see me from all sides. It doesn't feel threatening, but I increase my barriers just in case. I don't want her to get an accidental look into my mind. Through our bond, I can feel the guys do the same.

"Curious," the woman says loud enough for us to hear. "You really are a Goddess."

I frown. I was told that dragons insist on ceremony and traditions, yet she hasn't actually introduced herself yet, nor has she welcomed me. I assume she's someone important, but she's not behaving like it at all.

"Did you doubt that?" I ask, trying to keep my voice level. I don't want it to sound like a challenge. Well, maybe I do, but I'm wise enough not to.

"Of course I did. We were told you were a demigoddess, but a few days ago, one of our spies sent word that you have changed into a Goddess. I didn't think it possible."

"One of your spies?" This time, I can't help it sound like an accusation.

"Dear child, I hope you're not as naive as to think that I don't have spies in your Palace. I'd be a rather bad Queen if we hadn't."

I smile pleasantly. "Of course, I'm just surprised you openly talk about them. Most people like to keep the existence of spies a secret."

She waves a hand as if she's far above 'most people'. She probably is. The authority filling her aura is only rivalled by that of my mother, although hers has turned into an echo of what it used to be.

"Let's go inside," the woman says and turns without another word, heading towards the large doors at the other end of the courtyard. Agierth follows her closely, an arm still wrapped around the other woman's wide waist.

"Shall we?" I ask the guys and together, we walk behind the strange couple and into the dragon palace.

Chapter Four

The Dragon Palace isn't all that different from my mother's, except that everything is oversized. Dragon-sized, I guess. The ceilings are almost too high to see in the dim light created by hundreds of flaming torches on the wall. No floating lights here. It's all a little more rustic and old-fashioned than I'm used to, but it's impressive nonetheless.

The two women aren't waiting for us, and their tall legs give them an advantage, so I almost have to run to keep up with them.

"They're not very polite," Frost whispers from behind me, but his brother shushes him immediately.

There are people everywhere in here, guards standing in front of doors, courtiers milling around corners, watching us curiously. I love that only about half of the women wear dresses, the others loose trousers and tunics that look to be made of a shimmery linen fabric. A lot of the guards are women too, but I'm used to that from my mother's Palace.

Gender doesn't matter in a place where female Guardians can be created to be just as strong as the men.

Finally, we reach a set of doors that are more elaborate than all the others we've seen so far. A dragon head is carved into them, its eyes sharp and menacing. They seem to look at me, look *into* me, even though I know that it's only metal, not real.

The doors open without anyone physically pushing them inwards, and we follow the women into the throne room. It's empty, thank the Gods. I've got enough of people watching me like I'm a new museum specimen. Or maybe a new toy a dragon can nibble on.

There are two thrones on the dais, one large one that is made of... are those scales? It looks like the throne is covered in big shiny dragon scales in a variety of colours. It seems a little morbid to sit on the scales of other dragons, but who am I to judge. The other throne is smaller and a simple gold. Look at me, calling gold 'simple'. I've come a long way since I lived as a human.

The woman in the blue dress takes a seat in the scale throne while Agierth sits down on the smaller one. Wow, does that mean the woman who greeted us at the Gate is actually Royalty? They never said so. I wonder why.

"I am Dewi, the Dragon Goddess and ruler of this Realm, and I welcome you to my halls, Princess Wynter."

She suddenly speaks with a formality that was lacking when the talked to us earlier.

"Wait, you're a Goddess?" I blurt out before I can stop myself.

Dewi smiles. "Of course I am."

Why can't I sense that? I know what the aura of Gods looks like, but she is so very different from them.

To me, she looks like she's neither God, human, Guardian nor dragon shifter, but something entirely different. Strange, but it seems like for now, I'll have to take her at her word.

"I am Wynter, Heiress to the Winter Throne, and these are Storm, Frost, Arc and Crispin, my Guardians. It's a pleasure to meet you."

I'm not sure if it is indeed a pleasure, but I'm trying to be diplomatic. For now. Somehow, this Goddess is rubbing me the wrong way.

Dewi points to Agierth. "You've already met my favourite consort. We have not seen each other for a long time, so I'd like to keep this short. We have business to do."

Judging from the heated looks the Goddess is giving the other woman, I can imagine what that 'business' will look like. And did she say 'favourite' consort? Does that mean there are more? Well, I guess I have four men, so she can have as many women as she likes. I'm not one to judge.

I nod. "You called us here. What would you like to discuss?"

"I don't want to discuss anything," Dewi says haughtily. "If I am to support you in this war against the darkness, then I need to know that you're a true leader. I have a test for you."

The doors open behind us and I turn around. A very familiar woman is brought in, surrounded by guards. Ada.

I stifle a shout and smoothen my expression before looking back at the dais. Dewi is watching me, probably searching for weaknesses. I smile at her.

"I was hoping I'd get to see Ada while I'm here," I tell her lightly.

A shadow falls over her aura, the equivalent of a frown. "You're not here to see her. You're here to judge her for her crimes."

I look back at Ada. I can't see her face, but her clothes are tattered and she's limping slightly. Is she a prisoner here? That changes the entire situation. She's a citizen of my Realm, which means that she's my responsibility. Luckily, Dewi seems to think the same thing, although I'm not sure that's good.

The guards stop in front of the thrones, Ada looking thin and small between them. Where are her Guardians? And where is that bloody dragon shifter who got her into this mess?

She turns her head and looks at me. I wish I could see her face. Her aura is faint in places, not looking healthy at all. She's been through a lot, that much is clear.

"Ada of the Winter Realm, you stand accused of treason, murder and conspiring against the rulers of the Dragon Realm. In the absence of Queen Beira, her daughter is here to judge you. Should you be found guilty, the sentence will be executed here." A flaming sword suddenly appears in the hand of one of the guards. It's a clear sign that the sentence could be death. Dewi looks straight at me. "I hope you'll make the right decision."

I step forward until I'm closer to Ada. I send out some magic to check her for injuries. She's malnourished and her right ankle is sprained, but there's no serious damage. I heal her ankle with a single thought and smile when Ada gasps in surprise.

"Pain might influence her statements," I mutter, smiling to myself when Ada's aura becomes a little more solid. Good.

I lift my voice so Dewi can hear me. "Do you want to explain the charges or shall I let the accused tell me?"

"Treason because she ran from the Winter Realm without permission," Dewi explains in a bored tone, "and because she freed one of your prisoners. I assume you're aware of that."

I nod curtly and the dragon woman continues.

"She then came to my Realm and on her way to the palace, slaughtered several of my people. When she arrived here, she sought to dispose of our rulers and bring unrest to my lands."

"I helped you get your throne back," Ada hisses, saying something for the first time. "You wouldn't even sit there without me."

"Silence!" Dewi roars, her aura flashing dangerously. "You will not speak unless addressed."

I frown. Ada isn't one to lie, so if that's true... it doesn't make any sense. I need more information.

"Ada, I'm going to examine your mind," I announce so that everybody can hear. "That will be a lot quicker than having to listen to statements and having to decide whether you or someone else is lying."

The last bit is a jab at Dewi, and I hope she sees it as that.

"You can't do that," the Dragon Goddess splutters. "You don't have that ability."

The mystery deepens. "Who told you that?" I ask, but I think I already know. Yes. She points at Ada.

"You lied to me!" Dewi shouts, but Ada shakes her head.

"I swear, Wyn wasn't able to do that when I left. Arc was though, one of her companions."

I'm getting more and more confused by the whole situation. I don't have the patience to ask more questions though, so I cup Ada's face with my hands.

"Relax your mind," I tell her softly. "It won't hurt."

Dewi is saying something in the background, but I don't care. I drift into Ada's mind, being as gentle as possible as I push past old memories and thoughts to find her recent past.

T he dragon prisoner is staring at me, his eyes wide, his expression that of a very desperate man. "The dragons are under attack," he whispers, his voice rough and exhausted. "You need to let me out of here. They won't last much longer."

"You can't think I'd set you free," I reply in Ada's voice. "You're a madman, I shouldn't even be talking to you."

"Not mad," he whispers. "She's still in my mind. She's always in there, hurting me, telling me what to do. Right now she's not, though, and I can talk. I can think. I need to leave."

I laugh. "See, you're mad, I told you. I'd think that hearing voices is a symptom of madness even for dragons."

"She's real," he hisses. "She's in every single dragon's mind. She controls us, makes us angry. She makes us kill. She captured the Queen and now we're bound to her."

Before I can say anything, his eyes roll up in his head and he falls back against the wall, his body twitching. He's having another seizure. Maybe those are causing his madness. Maybe they're messing with his brain.

I sigh and continue writing my notes on his behaviour. I should be interrogating him, but it's no use. He either mutters nonsense, or he's too far out of it to even hear my questions. I can't make sense of him, and that bothers me.

"L isten! Listen to her!" He's pressed against the barrier, the palms of his hands so tight against it that his flesh has turned white.

"I can't hear her," I tell him softly. I've started to pity him. His pain doesn't seem to get any less and his seizures are increasing in intensity. "She's in your head."

"Yes, she is, now listen."

He squeezes a hand through the tiny opening in the glass barrier that's usually used to give him food. He wants me to touch him. No chance. I don't know what kind of tricks he's got up his sleeve. The cell is in a magic vacuum, so he can't shift or do magic, but despite his weakness and malnourished appearance, he's bigger than me.

"She isn't real," I tell him for the hundredth time. "I won't be able to hear her. Just ignore her and focus on the present."

"She's hurting my people," he growls, his eyes suddenly a little clearer. "I need to do something."

"I'm sure they'd have sent a message if they were in need of assistance," I tell him soothingly. "We'd know about it."

"You don't understand," he shouts in desperation. "She's in everybody's head! She controls everyone. We can't ask for help because she forbids it."

I sigh. We've been over this before. Many times.

"Let me show you," he begs, catching my gaze with his beautiful mahogany eyes. "Please."

I shouldn't. This is completely unprofessional. I should leave and let Arc and the Queen deal with him. But something in his expression makes me reach out and touch his hand.

A face flashes in my mind. A woman with hair as black as the night and eyes so cruel that it hurts to look at them.

I stumble back. "Who is she?"

S tepping back from Ada's mind, I take a deep breath and address the Dragon Queen. "The Morrigan was in control of all dragons?"

"How do you... You really can read minds," Dewi says in astonishment. Her aura changes from angry to something else.

I shrug. "I told you so. Where is the prisoner Ada set free?"

"In custody," Dewi snaps coldly. "He's my responsibility to deal with."

"And Ada's Guardians?"

"They followed her orders. They will be given the same sentence she gets."

There's no emotion in her voice. She doesn't care about these men in the slightest. Ada's aura is turning an angry white, so I intervene before she does something rash.

"Dewi, would you mind explaining what's happened or shall I continue looking through Ada's mind?"

Again, the Queen's aura flutters as if she's hiding something.

"I will explain," Agierth volunteers surprisingly. Dewi doesn't protest, which I find strange, but everything she's said and done so far has been confusing. I have no idea what to make of the Dragon Goddess.

Agierth gets up from her throne and squares her shoulder. "You're right. We were attacked by the Morrigan, and she took our Queen prisoner. Most people don't know that we're bound to our Queen, and she has power over us all. She rarely uses that gift, but the Morrigan exploited it. She twisted the beautiful magic that connects us and turned it into a prison for us all."

She falls quiet and the pieces fall into place. "The assassin, the dragon assassin... he was sent by the Morrigan? She made him do it?"

Agierth nods. "He didn't have a choice in the matter. He was a puppet, just a tool. Only when he got away from the Dragon Realm did her influence over him lessen enough that he could think clearly from time to time."

Yes, I saw that. Moments of clarity, interspersed with days of insanity.

"Then why is he a prisoner here?" I ask. "It wasn't his fault?"

"It's the principle," Dewi snaps. "He tried to assassinate a member of a Royal family."

Agierth puts a hand on the Queen's shoulder and to my surprise, their auras touch and merge at the seams. Maybe that's another strange dragon thing?

"The Guardians and Alastair came here and managed to free the Queen."

"It wasn't as easy as she makes it sound," Ada mutters and I have to suppress a grin.

"Wait, how did he manage to keep the Morrigan from controlling him? I thought her influence would get stronger again once he'd returned to this realm?" I ask and Agierth nods.

"They met someone. A unicorn."

"Blaze!" I exclaim. I hadn't realised he was this deeply involved.

"You know him?" Dewi asks in surprise.

"He's a friend of my men," I explain. "And mine too, I guess."

"I didn't think unicorns made friends," the Goddess replies coldly. Seriously, what is it with that woman? Why does she have that massive stick in her arse?

"Well, he's mine," I say just as coldly. "So you were the one captured?"

A black film spreads over Dewi's aura. Pain? Fear?

"Yes." Her voice is quiet all of a sudden. "I don't remember it."

I sigh. "You know what? I think we've moved on beyond silly games. Ada and her men will come back with me. Her dragon shifter too, if he wants. He'll be welcome in my Realm. Now, I assume you want revenge for what the Morrigan's done to you and your people. Be my guest. You're very welcome to join my battle against her. We'll be grateful for your help, but I'm not going to stand here and prove to you that I'm worthy. We're wasting precious time. I'm fighting the Morrigan, you want to, so I don't see any reason why we shouldn't join forces. If you decide you don't want to, then so be it."

I'm fuming inside, but I keep my voice calm and level.

Agierth and Dewi look at each other, their auras still touching. Are they bonded like I am to my Guardians? I can't see my own aura, so I don't know if ours looks the same. I hope it does. It seems like a beautiful connection.

"You have shown your claws," Dewi says gravely, "and we have seen them. We recognise your strength and we will follow you into battle."

Chapter Five

"It's good to be home," Ada sighs as she lets go of my arm. I've teleported us into my private quarters so we can have a proper chat. Her men are with her, immediately looking around the room as if they're expecting a threat. After all they've been through, it's no wonder they're a little skittish.

"You better stay here until I've announced that you're no longer wanted for treason," I say with a grin. "I don't want any vigilantes attacking you, thinking they're doing it for the good of the crown."

"Yes, good idea," one of her men growls. I can never tell them apart. They're triplets and with their uniforms, they look far too similar. Right now, those uniforms are dirty and ripped in places.

"Storm, would you mind looking after these gentlemen? I have a few things to discuss with Ada."

His aura swirls like he's about to protest, but he nods and takes them outside. The dragon prisoner follows - no, wait, he's no longer a prisoner. I guess he's an ally now. Hopefully, his craziness really has vanished.

"Want us to stay?" Arc asks but I shake my head.

"No, I want some girl time."

"That sounds like fun," Crispin snickers. "If you want some boy time after, we'll be in our quarters. Probably. Unless someone finds us and gives us something to do." He sighs. "No rest for the wicked."

They leave and I take a deep breath when we're finally alone. "How are you?" I ask Ada carefully, cursing my strange eyes that don't let me see her expression.

"It's strange to be back here," she says after a moment of hesitation. "At one point, I didn't think I'd ever be able to return."

"You've been through a lot, but I'm glad to have you back. I will need to have a chat with Gwain to discuss how to announce that you're back, but before you start work again, I want you to recover."

"I don't need...," she protests, but I cut her off.

"Yes, you do. You need some rest and proper food. I think you deserve some downtime, and so do your men. You all look like you'd collapse as soon as you're sent into battle."

"Your Majesty," she replies sullenly.

"Oh, stop it. I only want the best for you." I want to hug her, but right now, I need to be the Princess rather than the friend. If Ada could, she'd immediately go back to her duties, but I can't have her do that. She needs rest.

"But first, I have a few questions, if you don't mind."

She shrugs. "Go ahead."

"Can we trust the dragons?" It's a loaded question, but I need to know. Ada will be able to give me a better answer than my advisors.

"Dewi is an ungrateful bitch, but she wants revenge, so yes, I think we can," Ada replies. "And she's got Agierth to keep her in check. That one's quite a nice dragon and one of the few who managed to fight the Morrigan, if just a little. I can't promise you that they'll stay in touch after we defeat the Morrigan, but I think we can count on them for now."

I smile. Finally some good news. It seems that the strange trip to the Dragon Realm was worth it after all, despite all the weirdness.

"It's good to have you back." Again, I have to stop myself from hugging her. I'm all giddy and excited, and I'm not quite sure why. Probably my hormones, or my weird Goddess powers. They keep doing strange stuff to me. I clear my throat. "Hold my hand, I'll get you to your quarters the quick way."

"How come you can teleport now?" she asks in wonder, as if she didn't quite realise that I already transported them back from the Dragon Realm in this way.

I sigh. "It's a long story."

My mother's condition hasn't improved at all. She's as pale as the bed sheets surrounding her frail body, and her cheeks seem sunk in even further than I remember. She's the only person whose face I can see, yet I don't want to look at her. She's changed too much, she's nothing but a shadow of the powerful Goddess she used to be. And it's all my fault. I made her use up all her powers. I behaved like a child and she's the one who's suffering for it.

"Beira?" I whisper, sitting down by her bedside. I wish there was something I could do. I have all these new powers now, but they're no use to me. I can't heal my mother.

She opens her eyes, but even that looks like a struggle for her.

"Wyn."

Her voice is less than a whisper, a weak breath. How did it come to this?

"Do you have news?" she asks, her eyes fluttering shut again.

I take her hand and squeeze it reassuringly. As if that will solve anything. It's more to give me comfort rather than her.

"The dragons will fight on our side," I tell her. "And Ada has returned. She never abandoned us, she left to help the dragon prisoner free his people from the Morrigan's influence. It's a long story, but for now, we have new allies."

I don't want to take up too much of my mother's energy by telling her the full line of events. It seems hard enough for her to stay awake.

"I'm proud of you," she whispers. "You've achieved something I haven't managed for centuries. The dragons have always been elusive."

"Their leader, Dewi, said she was a Goddess, but she didn't feel like other Gods. Do you know about her?"

My mother frowns ever so slightly. "She's not one of mine. Maybe Angus made her, but I've never heard of a Dragon Goddess."

"Strange," I mutter, more to myself than to her. "She's not making any sense."

"Wyn." My mother suddenly squeezes my hand, making me turn my full attention to her again.

"You need to become Queen."

I sigh. "Not that again. No way. You'll be better once we've defeated Angus, and then you won't need me anymore."

"I won't get better," she says slowly. "My time is over."

I shake my head. "I'm not listening. Once winter comes again, you'll be just like you were before."

"No, I can feel it. I won't recover, Wyn, no matter how much you want it. Even if I get stronger, I'll never get back to my old strength. I won't be able to lead my people. I won't be the Queen they deserve."

A tear is trickling from the corner of her eye and I look away. Beira doesn't cry. She's the Winter Queen, the epitome of cool composure. She doesn't show her emotions, ever.

"You need to be crowned before the battle begins." Her grip on my hand is growing weaker, but her voice has a trace of her former authority. "We will all die if you don't become Queen."

She falls silent and I stare at the floor, her words echoing in my head. She won't get better. She won't be Beira again. She'll stay this weak, frail woman, not much more than human.

"There needs to be a balance," she suddenly whispers, just when I think she's gone back to sleep. "Remember what I told you. Without balance, all Realms will crumble. I can already feel it happening. Focus, and you'll feel it too."

. . .

I sit by her side for a while longer, even though she's asleep. I think I know how to feel for the balance like she said, but I'm scared to do it. If I sense an imbalance, that will mean that I will have to do something about it.

I don't want to be Queen. I don't want to be a Goddess, either. All I want is to go back to being Wyn, live with my Guardians, have a quiet life without death and demons. I want my mum and my mother by my side, and a father who isn't traumatised and grieving.

I never imagined my life could turn into this. Chaos. War. Despair. Doubt. An eternal absence of hope. And now, they want me to be Queen and steer them through the darkness. What if I fail? What if I get them all killed? I could never live with that. There's been too much death already. Mum. Chesca. Aodh. All the soldiers we've lost.

But for it to end, we need to fight, and my mother is right. She can't lead us in the state she's in.

I run my hands through my long hair, wishing there was a simple answer. Why can't life be simple, just once? I think I've dealt with my share fair of heartache and trouble, why can't it be someone else's turn now?

No, that's not a way a Princess should think. I should be happy to take on the responsibility and suffering that comes with my role, as long as it means my people are safe. But am I ready to be that person? Can I put all my own worries to one side and completely focus on what's good for my Realm?

Already, I don't have enough time to spend with my Guardians. I bet that as Queen, I'd have even less. I miss them, I miss our closeness, our banter. I can feel them through our bond, but that's no substitute for having them in the room with me.

Urgh. My head hurts with all the thoughts swirling around my mind.

The balance... I remember what my mother told me when I'd first arrived in the Realm. How she and Angus share their rule of the world, how he makes plants grow and thrive in the summer, and how Beira give them their well-earned rest during the winter months. Nature has got used to the rhythm that they've maintained over millennia, and if that balance was to be disturbed, all of creation might be affected. She'd said that magic might no longer exist in a world without the precarious balance that she'd fought for despite Angus trying to extend his powers. She's fought him before, many times, and each time, she won, but she never took away his Realm and his powers. He's needed for the balance, and even now, I know that we can't defeat him completely, only drive him back. Who we need to defeat is the Morrigan, who doesn't seem to care about the damage this war between Winter and Summer could cause. She'd probably enjoy it. If she lives in the Demon Realms now, I bet she'd be happy with a world of darkness and despair.

I look at Beira again. Her lover, my father, was killed by Angus's soldiers, and yet she still tried to keep the peace. I'm not sure I'd be able to do that if someone killed my men. Scratch that, I certainly wouldn't. I'd want to make Angus suffer in the worst possible way.

Yet another reason why I'd make a terrible Queen. I'm too emotional, too human. Maybe if I'd grown up here in the Realms, it could have been different, but I didn't.

To Queen or not to Queen... I smirk at my own bad joke. Everybody is telling me to do it. The Council, Tamara, even my father. And my Guardians. This is the first time they're not supporting my decision. Storm is particularly adamant that I should take my mother's place. But they're part of this Realm, no wonder they think like everybody here. Am I the only one who can see what a bad idea it is?

I'm not the right person for the job.

I sigh. Sitting here lamenting my fate won't do any good. I better get going, there's a Council to inform about the dragons, and I'm pretty sure there's a mountain of documents to sign waiting for me on my desk.

Chapter Six

Before I can even get to my office, Tamara waylays me.

"There's something you should see," she tells me, the urgency in her voice surprising me. She's usually very well composed and while she likes to laugh, she very rarely shows any other emotions.

"What's going on?"

"It's the unicorn. He's having... I don't know, it looks like he's having a seizure. He's saying strange things and his body is twitching. I've sent for Theodore and Zephyr, but you know the unicorn better than any of us.

"Where is he?" I ask, fear filling my stomach. I can't deal with another loss.

"Practice courtyard. He went there to..."

I'm already gone, teleporting there before Tamara can finish her sentence.

. . .

It's chaos in the courtyard. A crowd has assembled, surrounding Blaze as he writhes on the ground. His beautiful white coat is dirty all over. He must have been rolling around on the gravel for a while.

"What happened?" I ask loudly and the crowd falls silent, quickly opening a passage so I can reach the unicorn.

A Guardian steps forward, only wearing a pair of loose trousers. His chest is sleek with sweat; he must have been training here when it happened.

"He was eating, or at least that's what he said he was doing, when he suddenly whinnied and collapsed. We tried to help him up, but then he started convulsing. Whenever he stops moving, he says the same words."

"Which are?" I ask sharply when he doesn't continue immediately.

"Spring dies, Summer falls, betrayed by darkness. Autumn's missing. Winter's called to help." He shrugs as if that doesn't make sense at all.

"That's all?"

"At the beginning, he muttered something about balances, but maybe I misheard him."

That's all too much of a coincidence. My mother tells me that the balance needs to be kept intact, and a moment later, Blaze does the same thing? Maybe this is just an elaborate plot to make me accept the crown.

The unicorn whinnies in pain and I immediately know how wrong I am. This isn't a plot. This is real.

I approach him, staying out of reach of his twitching hooves.

"Blaze? Can you hear me?"

He suddenly grows still, his ears twitching.

"Touch my horn," he rasps, his eyes rolling back and forth like he has no control about them.

I hesitate for a moment, but then do as he asks, grabbing his horn, still making sure to stay away from his shaking legs.

A flash of rainbow light assaults my senses and then I'm floating, no longer in the courtyard. I know this place...

"Where are we?"

I swirl around and stare at Blaze. The unicorn is looking as healthy as ever, his fur shimmering in the colourful light surrounding us.

"You don't know?"

"We're in your head, silly. This is your dream, not mine."

I blush. "When I first stepped through the Gate at the Calanais Stones, I ended up on a rainbow. *This* rainbow." I don't tell him that I also had sex on this very rainbow. It's already embarrassing enough to be back here, in the tackiest place in the universe.

"I like it," he says cheerfully. "You've got taste."

"Shut up and explain what's happening."

He whinnies. "So impatient. But you're right, we don't have much time. My body won't be able to deal with the magic overdose for much longer without your help."

"Magic overdose?"

He paws the ground, looking a little sheepish. "I overate."

"Seriously? You ate too much and now you're having seizures?"

"It was on purpose."

I shake my head, incredulous. "You wanted this to happen?"

"When I get gorged on magic, I get visions. Sometimes, not always, but in a place as full of magic as this Palace, I thought it was worth a try."

I sigh. "And you couldn't have warned someone about it?"

"You weren't there," he complains. "And I didn't think it would happen this quickly. Now, when we go back, you need to listen exactly to what I say. I can't always remember, so don't expect me to tell you afterwards. Then, you need to pull the excess magic out of my body. It might make you feel a little weird, though."

"Weird? How?"

He blushes in his strange unicorn way. "Remember sparklies?"

"No. No way!"

I step away from Blaze, glaring at him.

"It's the only way. Just make sure that someone gets you out of sight quickly." He grins. "Especially now that you've decided you're going to be Queen."

"I have not," I protest, but he groans.

"Time to go back. Remember, listen to what I say. Write it down, if you have to. Then get the magic out of me. It hurts."

Before I can say anything, the rainbow light flashes again and I'm back in the courtyard, stumbling away from the unicorn who's still on the ground, his entire body twitching.

"Get my Guardians!" I shout at one of the onlookers. "Now!"

They hurry away and I turn back to Blaze.

"Quiet, everyone! Listen to what he says and write it down if you can," I command, and silence falls. The entire crowd is waiting to hear what Blaze is about to say. I hope he's actually going to say something, otherwise I won't have a clue what to do.

"Spring is taken," he suddenly groans. "Spring is taken. Summer will be betrayed. Where is Autumn? Find Autumn or Winter will thaw. The balance must be maintained. Darkness is coming, there's no escape."

He whinnies in pain and falls silent. Froth is forming around his mouth as his body begins to seize again. I close my eyes and focus on the magic around him. He's a beautiful sight, his entire body made of magic, colourful and bright. Right now though, it's sparking all over the place, like electricity that's about to turn into lightning.

I start to funnel some of the excess magic away from Blaze and into myself. Maybe I should disperse it into the environment, but who knows what unicorn magic might cause if it's set free. It's not like I have any experience with this kind of magic. Except for sparklies. I really hope my Guardians will be there to take me away. If my previous reactions to the unicorn drug are anything to go by, it will be embarrassing as hell.

When I've pulled enough magic away from him - at least I hope so - I open my eyes again. Blaze has stopped twitching and is breathing heavily instead.

I kneel by his side. "Blaze?"

He slowly opens one eye. "Sleep."

I smile. "Sleep as long as you need to."

I get up again and turn to the crowd. "I want someone to stay with him until he can get up by himself. If there's any change, you notify me immediately." Two Guardians bow and take up positions on either side of the unicorn, looking ready to fight off both enemies and curious onlookers. I'm still surprised at the fervour with which people carry out my commands nowadays.

So far, I'm not noticing any effect of the unicorn magic. Maybe I'm strong enough to withstand it now. I concentrate on the magic inside of me. She's sleeping in her cave, her head almost touching the ceiling. She's grown so much, but I don't know how to make the cave bigger. A cloud of rainbow dust is swirling around her. Blaze's magic, just as eccentric and flamboyant as he is. One day, I hope I'm going to meet other unicorns so I can find out whether he's special even among his own species, or whether they're all like him.

I smile at the thought of seeing a herd of unicorns. Do they have herds? I think they're too solitary for that. But still, maybe Blaze has family he could introduce me to. Siblings? Parents? Baby unicorns? I would love to cuddle a baby unicorn. Are they born with horns or do they grow later? I hope the latter, otherwise I imagine the birth to be pretty painful for the mother unicorn.

"I think it's time ta leave," a gentle voice says behind me and I turn to find my Guardians waiting for me. They're forming a line, blocking my view of the rest of the crowd.

"Leave? Why?" I ask in confusion.

Arc laughs. "I dinnae think people want ta hear yer thoughts about baby unicorns." He steps forwards and sweeps me into his arms. "Yer very cute when yer stoned."

"Wyn, can you teleport us to your quarters?" Storm asks and I nod enthusiastically. Nothing better than being in my rooms with my men.

I transport us into my bedroom.

"I think ya forgot the others," Arc grins as soon as we've arrived.

Oh. Yes. Oops.

"Sorry."

"Was it intentional?" he asks, turning me so I face him. His hands on my shoulders feel good, so good. I want to feel them everywhere.

I shrug. "Maybe? Don't know. Dinnae ken."

"Did ya just mock my accent?"

I shrug again. "Maybe?"

"If I was Storm, I'd punish ya for that. But I'm not. I just want ta kiss ya."

I smile. He's so nice. So pretty. His magic is pretty. His aura is sparkling. I want him so much.

"Do it."

He doesn't need another invitation. He wraps his arms around my waist and pulls me close until my chest touches his. His chest is hard, mine isn't. My boobs are soft, although my nipples are getting harder. They want him, just like the rest of me. I giggle, but Arc shuts me up with his lips.

Yummy. I kiss him back and hug him tight. Well, I'm hugging his arse, but that's okay. He's firm and hard there, too, and there's even more hardness pressing against my belly.

His tongue is tracing my lips, tickling me. I laugh against his kiss, the happiness bubbling out of me. I want to hug the entire world. Everything is so nice, so pretty. On the other side of the room, the door opens and my other three Guardians enter. I can feel them. I pull at the bond connecting me to them and all three of them gasp. Funny.

"What did you do that for?" Frost complains. "It feels weird."

Arc stops kissing me so I can reply. Bad Arc. I want him to continue.

"I want to hug you," I announce and take my hands off Arc's arse so I have space for all my Guardians.

"She's totally out of it," Crispin mutters. "I'm glad we got there in time."

"Me too," Storm says, his voice surprisingly dark.

"Don't be dark," I tell him. "Be happy. Like rainbows."

"See what I mean?" Storm sighs. "I'm going to kill that unicorn. Slowly."

"Blaze made me happy," I protest and Arc laughs, his chest vibrating against mine.

"We can see that, lass. Yer very happy."

I nod. "I am. Are you happy too?"

"Yer in my arms, of course I'm happy." He lowers his head to kiss me again, but I'm not finished talking yet. I bite his lower lip to make sure he knows.

"Ouch, what was that for!"

"I need to talk," I tell him.

"Crispin, can you do something about this?" Storm asks. He sounds as if he's in pain.

I wriggle out of Arc's embrace and run to Storm, hugging him instead.

"What's wrong?" I ask him in concern. "Where does it hurt?"

"Hurt? What?" He sighs again. "It doesn't hurt. Everything's fine."

I smile at him. "Good, then we can kiss. Kissing is fun."

Frost roars in laughter, distracting me from my kissing plans.

"I only have one mouth," I observe. "How am I going to kiss all of you?"

"We can take turns," Arc suggests. He's joined us and now, all four Guardians are surrounding me.

"We can, after she's come down from this high," Storm says sternly. "We're not going to do anything while she doesn't have control over herself."

"No, I want to kiss," I complain. "I want Arc's hardness."

Frost is on the floor, laughing, and Crispin is bent over as well, looking like he's having trouble breathing.

"You can have it later, I promise." Storm lifts me up and carries me over to the bed.

"Are we going to have sex?" I ask excitedly, but to my disappointment, he shakes his head.

"No, you're going to lie here and sleep for a bit, until the unicorn magic is out of your system. Then we can do whatever we want."

"But I want it now," I moan. "I need you."

"We're not going to take advantage of you in this state. Sleep and we'll be there when you wake up." He lies down beside me to emphasise his point.

Good. He's close enough for me to reach out and touch his -

"Do I need to tie you up?" he growls, turning onto his back to protect himself from my grabby hands.

"I love being tied up," I say full of enthusiasm. "Tying up is fun."

"Crispin, please?" Storm asks, holding my wrists as I try to get close to him again.

The healer chuckles and appears at my other side, distracting me from trying to open Storm's jeans. He puts a hand on my forehead, so soft, so cool.

"Sleep, Wyn," he whispers and a warm hug surrounds me, helping me drift off away from my rainbow thoughts.

Chapter Seven

Embarrassment floods my mind. Then, words.

"Spring is taken. Summer will be betrayed. Where is Autumn? Find Autumn or Winter will thaw. The balance must be maintained. Darkness is coming, there's no escape."

I whisper the words before they flee my mind.

"What?" Crispin mutters sleepily into my ear. His head is snuggled against my shoulder, his breath hot against my cheek.

"Blaze said that when he was in his food coma."

My Guardian sits up, choking with laughter. "Is that what it was? He ate too much?"

I grin. "Yup. Too much magic. Although he said that he did it intentionally to get a vision. Apparently, unicorns can do that. He told me to keep a note of what he prophesied, but I think my mind went a little weird after that."

"You could say that," Crispin laughs. "You were rather cute."

I shove my elbow into his thigh and he laughs even more.

"It was even better than the first time he gave you sparklies. Priceless, really."

I tousle his hair with my magic and he yelps, slapping a hand on his head as if he's expecting there to be spiders.

I sit up as well, noticing that I'm still wearing the same dress I wore to travel to the Dragon Realm. Was that only this morning?

"What time is it?" I ask, even though I know that my magic could probably tell me.

"Three in the morning. We didn't know how long the unicorn effect would last, so I made you sleep a bit longer than probably necessary."

"Thanks." I smile at him.

"You're not mad?"

I cringe. "For not letting me behave like an idiot? No, better to knock me out. You've hereby got permission to do it again next time."

Crispin chuckles. "With pleasure. Although I hope you're not planning to expose yourself to sparklies again soon."

"Nope, definitely not. This was an emergency. And now that I can actually think, it was a good idea that Blaze did this. 'Spring is taken.' I think we should find out if anything has happened in the Spring Realm. Flora is still here in the Palace, right?"

He nods. "As far as I'm aware. I think I saw her in the Great Hall at dinner yesterday."

I sigh. I really want to stay in bed with Crispin, do some of the things I planned to do with the guys while I was drugged, but the weight of responsibility is making me get up.

"I better pay her a visit. Want to come?"

Crispin shakes his head. "I'll go and see if there are any new reports from the Spring Realm. Meet in your office?"

"Yes, let's hope this was either just unicorn nonsense, or hasn't happened yet."

I teleport away from my chambers and to the guest rooms. I'm not quite sure what rooms Flora has been assigned, so I appear at the main door leading to the guest wing. The two guards jump and shout, but immediately bow when they see me.

"Sorry, Your Highness," one of them apologises. "I didn't know it was you."

"Lead me to the Spring Goddess," I say without engaging in small talk. "It's urgent."

The guard nods and opens the door, motioning me to follow. The guest wing is extensive and spread over several floors with enough rooms to house hundreds of people. Not all Gods can teleport, and after a long night of drinks and delights, some like to stay here rather than travel to the closest Gate. Having a room also helps when meeting a pretty Guardian to take to bed.

Luckily, Flora's quarters aren't far. The guard gives me a questioning look and I tell him to return to his post.

I wait until he's gone before knocking on the door. There's no response, but it's the middle of the night, so I didn't expect Flora to be awake.

I knock again, then enter the dark room. With a thought, I switch on the lights. I'm in a cosy living room, made homely by dozens of flower vases dotted around the shelves and tables. It's obvious that the Spring Goddess has tried to make this place more like home. She must miss her own Realm, which according to what she's said looks very different from this one. More colours, less snow, obviously.

"Flora?" I call as a warning before heading towards the door at the end of the room. I don't want to scare her.

Actually, I could just use my magic. Silly me, I'm still not used to it. I concentrate on my surroundings, feeling for nearby auras. There's nobody here. Damn it.

I run and open the bedroom door, but as I thought, it's empty. The bed looks like nobody has slept in tonight, but there are boxes and clothes everywhere, so she's definitely been living in here. Maybe she's out partying or has found a lover. I refuse to think that it's something more sinister.

I teleport back to the entrance to the guest wing. This time, the guards don't shriek quite as much.

"When did you last see Flora?" I ask immediately and they look at each other.

"Yesterday," one of them says and the other nods. "She came back here after dinner, and a few minutes later, one of your Guardians came to pick her up."

"One of my Guardians?" I ask, a sinking feeling spreading through my stomach. Please don't let this happen again.

"Crispin, Your Highness," the other guard supplies. "He said you'd requested Lady Flora's presence."

I teleport away from them, into my office. As soon as I'm there, I pull on the bond connecting me to my Guardians. I try to avoid doing this because they don't like the feeling of it, but I need them here, now, and I don't have time to search for them.

I open the door and tell one of the guards outside to send for Tamara. If she's surprised that I'm in the office without them having seen me walk through the door, she doesn't show it. I guess they're used to it from my mother.

"My Guardians will be here any minute. You can let them in without asking." She nods and bows her head.

I close the door behind me and look around my empty office. Yet again, I have a crisis to master, and yet again, my mother isn't here to help me. It's depressing.

Arc is the first to arrive, bursting into the room. "What happened?" he huffs, completely out of breath. He must have run here.

"Flora is gone, but let's wait for the others. We have another fake Crispin on the loose."

"Another one?" He flops down on one of the chairs. "Wasn't everyone told about the possibility of one of them reappearing?"

I sigh. "Apparently not, or he knew the passcode. I'll have to ask the guards. Actually, wait here for the others, I'll be right back."

I teleport back to the guest wing. The same two guards are still standing there.

"When Crispin picked up Flora, did you ask him for the code word?" I ask them sharply, half expecting them to admit that they didn't, but the burly one to the right bows.

"Of course, Your Highness. He answered correctly." He pauses for a moment, exchanging a look with his colleague. "Does that mean that it was an impostor?"

I nod. "It seems that way. For now, spread the word that the real Crispin will stay by my side, so if he is spotted without me, sound the alarm."

I disappear before they can respond, trusting them to follow my command.

Back in the office, Crispin and Storm have joined Arc. I can't help myself, I scan Crispin's aura to make sure that it's really him.

"I checked," Arc mutters. "It's Crisp."

"The one and only," Crispin says darkly. "Sorry for giving you so much trouble."

I go to him and pull him up from his chair, taking him into my arms. "It's not your fault," I whisper into his ear. "None of this is your fault."

He shakes his head as if he doesn't agree, but that's when Frost runs into the room, panting heavily. "What's up?"

Behind him is Tamara, a net covering her grey hair. She looks even more grandmotherly in her bright purple dressing gown and her fluffy slippers.

I step back from Crispin, wishing once again that I could see his face. His aura is dark and broody, full of sadness and regret. Does it show in his expression? In his eyes?

I take a deep breath and face my audience. "The Spring Goddess has disappeared. The guards saw Crispin lead her away, and as *my* Crispin didn't do that, we have to assume that we have another clone in the Palace. Crispin, from now on you're going to stay by my side so that if your clone is seen on his own, everybody knows that it's an impostor.

"Guess that's one way of spending more time with you," he says under his breath, but I don't have time to reply. There's too much at stake here.

"Flora's disappearance fits with what Blaze said during his vision."

"Is that what it was?" Tamara interrupts. "A vision? I didn't know unicorns had that power."

I shrug. "Neither did I, but apparently, they do. He said that Spring would be taken, and that's exactly what happened. We need to find Flora, but there's more we need to be aware of."

"Summer will be betrayed," Crispin recites. "Find Autumn or Winter will thaw. The balance must be maintained. Darkness is coming, there's no escape."

"Does that mean the Morrigan will betray Angus?" Tamara asks, hope swinging in her voice.

"That would be nice," I mutter, "but life hasn't been very nice recently. Maybe there's going to be betrayal inside the Realm? Maybe his wife will betray him? Who knows. For now, I think we need to focus on Flora and Autumn."

I've put off asking the most important question for now because I don't want to show my ignorance. I thought I'd learned quite a bit about the Gods and Goddesses by now, but once again, my lack of knowledge is showing. Well, no way around it.

"Who's the God of Autumn?" I ask, kicking myself internally. Such a stupid question. I should know this. "Or is it a Goddess?"

"There isn't one," Storm replies with a shrug. "Never has been."

"Wait, so there are Gods for Spring, Summer and Winter, but not for Autumn? Isn't that a bit discriminatory?"

"I'm not sure you can discriminate against a season," Frost jokes. "I think there was never a need for one. In autumn, Beira takes over from Angus and slowly introduces winter to all life. In spring, she retreats, but during winter, some beings die, so the Spring Goddess is needed to breathe new life into the worlds, before passing the baton on to Angus."

That doesn't really make sense to me, but alright, so there's no official Autumn God.

"I think Blaze disagrees with that," I point out. "He says to find Autumn. How can we find a God that doesn't exist?"

"Maybe it's a riddle," Tamara suggests. "Perhaps we shouldn't be taking it literally."

"What else could it mean, though?" Storm asks. Nobody answers, we're all just as clueless.

"Autumn... harvest... end of summer...," I mutter more to myself than to the others. "Beginning of winter... third season of the year..."

"Wait," Frost says, his aura brightening. "Beginning of winter. Winter. Maybe it's a hint that you should be crowned?"

I sigh. "Please don't interpret things into this that don't make sense. I know you all want me to take the throne, but that's not your decision to make."

"But don't you see?" His enthusiasm confuses me. "We'd be crowning Autumn. Not Winter. Your mother wouldn't have to give up the throne if we don't crown Winter, but Autumn."

I shake my head. "As lovely as that sounds, this Realm needs a Winter Queen, not an Autumn one."

"Ha!" Tamara explains. "You said it needs a Queen. Finally."

"Stop it, all of you." I grimace. "This is not up for discussion."

"End of the warmth, beginning of the cold," Crispin says quietly. "Fire and Ice. I think we may have already found Autumn."

My heart is starting to beat faster as I realise what he means. "Dewi? The Dragon Goddess?"

Crispin nods. "Maybe I'm just trying to make it easy for us, but it would make sense. They are ice dragons living in a hot Realm. It's like the changing of the seasons, having both temperatures at once."

"Wouldn't my mother know about her, though? I can't believe a Goddess can just stay under the radar for so long, especially if she's representing one of the seasons."

"About that," Tamara says and pulls a book from her dressing gown's pocket. "After you mentioned Dewi, I decided to do some research. She's mentioned in here, but not as a Goddess."

She hands me the book, knowing that I'll be able to read its entire contents within seconds. I lay my hand on its cover and take a deep breath, before letting the knowledge stream into me.

"Oh."

"Exactly," Tamara confirms. "Are you thinking what I'm thinking?"

"What is it?" Storm asks impatiently.

I smile. "Dewi is described as a demigoddess in here, the daughter of a dragon shifter and an unnamed God. She was raised away from the Realms and grew up amongst dragons. Now she's a Goddess. Remind you of someone?"

Their auras are shifting when they realise what it means. "She's like you," Frost gasps. "A demigoddess turned Goddess. That means she could be Autumn, but because the dragons are so reclusive, nobody has named her as such. That also explains why Beira didn't know about her."

I nod. "Exactly. I think we've found our Autumn, and luckily, she's already on our side. Finally some good news."

"Find Autumn or Winter will thaw," Crispin recites again. "That means that without her help, we would probably have lost the battle. That doesn't mean that we'll win it though, even with the dragons. It's not going to be easy."

"Aye, and Spring is missing. We need ta find Flora." Arc has been quiet until now, which is unusual for him, but I don't have the time to worry about it.

"Yes, our priority right now is to find the Spring Goddess and any Crispin clones that might still be in the Palace. Storm, you're in charge of the search. Arc and Frost will help you. Tamara, please inform the Council and our allies."

"What about me?" Crispin asks, a shadow surrounding the rims of his aura. He doesn't want to be left out.

"You're with me," I tell him with a smile. "There's something I need to do."

Chapter Eight

I teleport us to the top of the highest tower. I don't think I need to be outside, or all the way up here, but it makes me feel a little more confident about what I'm about to try.

"Want to explain what we're doing here?" Crispin asks, walking to the edge of the tower and looking down. It's still dark, but a thin slice of dawn is appearing on the horizon behind him. Soon, the sun will rise and a new day will begin.

"I need to feel the balance," I say quietly, hoping that it doesn't sound too silly. "Both my mother and Blaze mention it, and Beira said that I could somehow *feel* it. I need to know how bad things are."

He nods. "How can I help?"

"Keep watch. I don't want to be surprised by overenthusiastic guards or assassins."

Crispin chuckles. "Are you putting guards and assassins in the same category now?"

"They're both annoying." I shrug. "Spoken like a true Princess, ey?"

He laughs. "Indeed. Don't worry, I won't let anyone disturb you."

"Thanks. And if I start muttering prophecies like Blaze, please ignore them. I've had enough cryptic advice for one day."

He laughs again, his aura turning a beautiful gold. In another life, I'd hug and kiss him right now, but I'm not that Wyn anymore. I can't be.

I sit down on the cold marble and cross my legs. Maybe I should start chanting om to make this even more ridiculous? I have no idea what I'm doing.

My mother's voice echoes through my mind. *Without balance, all Realms will crumble. I can already feel it happening. Focus, and you'll feel it too.*

I close my eyes and take a few deep, slow breaths. I've never been good at sitting still. As soon as I do, I think of something that needs doing, or of something I really want to do. But this is important. Focus, Wyn. Focus.

I concentrate on my breath without actually changing it. In, out. In, out. The air flows into me, and then out again, connecting me to the world outside. I can hear Crispin behind me, breathing the same air. Everyone in this Palace is breathing in and out, everyone, everywhere. I feel connected to them through this simple, essential motion.

In and out. It's a balance that cannot be disturbed. We need to breathe the air in as much as we need to breathe it back out. It's a constant cycle, as steady as the seasons. There cannot be summer without winter.

Slowly, my awareness widens and I feel the magic around me in a different way. It's pulsing, moving in patterns that I hadn't recognised before. Swirls, knots and parallel lines. There's a message in the patterns, a simple warning that reverberates throughout everybody's lifeforce.

Preserve.

The magic is only a small part of a bigger picture though. I expand my senses further until I reach the underlying forces that feed the magic. Life and death. Yet another balance, but this one is tainted. It's hurting and wanting me to help it, but I don't know how. There's more death than life, and it's changing rapidly. With the upcoming battle, this imbalance is only going to get worse. We need more life so that the balance is restored, but how's that supposed to be achieved? I can't just tell everyone to get more babies? No, we need to do it the other way round. Prevent more deaths.

I float further away, towards the circle of seasons. They're based on life and death, and yet they are so much more. Winter isn't just death, it's also renewal, preservation, recovery. Summer is life and decay, beauty and droughts. Then there's autumn and spring, times of change and transition. Again, there's death and life in both of them. Only when all four are put together can life thrive. I'd never seen it so clearly, but now I know deep in my heart what others have been trying to tell me. Winter needs to be strong to match the power of the summer. It's not a matter of weakening summer, no, that would go against the balance. It's about putting all of them on equal footing.

I let myself fall into the magic, soaking up the feeling of anguish that's streaming from the imbalance. Cracks are already appearing in the fabric of life, and I know that if nothing is done, magic will start to be drawn out of the tears into nothingness. We'll be left powerless, all of us, no matter which Realm we live in. There won't be magic, and without magic, there's no life and death. Images flash into my mind. Babies crying, blood dripping from never-closing wounds, lovers torn apart. Forests burning, lakes drying up, harvests too small to feed families. The world is hurting and nobody is doing anything about it. In contrary, we're making it worse.

Help is needed, and help will come. "I'll make this right," I promise. "The balance will be restored."

A feeling of gratefulness spreads within me, and I know it isn't my own emotion. More images are thrown into my mind, but these are different. They're hope.

I open my eyes and close them again right away, blinded by the sun. How is there so much daylight already?

"Are you awake again?" Crispin asks sleepily. He's sat against the battlement, watching me.

"How long was I... away?"

"Must have been at least three hours. Your breathing became really slow, I was worried for a bit. It was like you went into a coma, but then you stabilised."

I swallow hard. Three hours. "We better get back, I'm sure the others are missing us already."

"The sunrise was beautiful," Crispin says softly, his aura turning a little blue in the centre. "I wonder how many more of them we'll be able to see."

I get up and walk over to him, holding out a hand. "An eternity. We won't let ourselves be defeated, and we'll send the

Morrigan back into the dark hole she crawled out of. This isn't the end, Crispy. It's only the beginning of our life together."

He looks up at me and for a moment, I get to see his eyes, a flash of emotion that makes me stumble. Then his aura covers his face again and I'm left breathing hard at the adoration I saw in his gaze.

"I love it when you call me Crispy," he chuckles. "But don't tell the others that."

I laugh. "I'll take it to the grave. No, let me rephrase that. I'll keep it a secret for eternity."

"You better. I don't think my enemies will cower in fear when they hear that you call me Crispy."

"Do they actually cower in fear?"

He shrugs. "You never know. Those clones might actually help in getting me a fearsome reputation." His aura darkens a little. "Again."

To distract him, I grip his hands and pull him up, using a bit of magic to give me enough strength. He's the least bulky of the four of them, but that doesn't mean he's small. Or light. "We should return to the others. Crispy."

"I know." He sighs. "I wish we could just stay up here and enjoy the sunshine together."

"After all this is over, I'm going to take a month off and spend it with all of you," I promise. "The Realm will just have to look after itself."

The darkness in his aura disappears. "We could travel the Realms," he says full of enthusiasm. "I could show you some amazing places."

"It's good to have something to look forward to. We'll get there, eventually. Only one idiot God and one evil bitch to defeat. How hard could that be."

Of course, nobody has seen fake Crispin and Flora. It would have surprised me; the Morrigan is far too clever for that. They're probably in her Realm by now, the Spring Goddess a prisoner or worse.

"We need to bring her back," Gwain says gravely, his hand gripping the hilt of his sword. "We failed in protecting her."

He and Tamara are standing in front of my desk, both looking grim and exhausted.

"We did, but we can't bring her back." I lift a hand when they start to protest. "I've seen what's at stake. Now that we have Autumn on our side - that's the Dragon Goddess, Gwain, I'll explain later - Angus needs to have Spring. The balance is already disturbed enough, and we can't injure it any further."

"But she's our ally!" Gwain protests. "We promised her she'd be safe."

I nod sadly. "Yes, we did. I did, and it's my responsibility. Believe me, I feel just as bad about this as you do, if not worse. A lot worse." I get up from my chair and look them straight in the eyes - not that I can actually see them, but I hope they don't notice that.

"I know what I need to do to restore peace, starting with my coronation."

Tamara can't stifle a small gasp. "You've changed your mind? How?"

"I've seen what happens if I don't do it," I say, trying to keep the bitterness from my voice. "I still don't agree with it, but I know that I have to do it. I have to become Queen."

Gwain bows deeply. "Your Majesty."

"Not quite yet." I shake my head. "But I will have to be, soon. Tamara, I know you've been itching to organise the coronation. I assume you've already taken preparations without my knowledge?"

"Of course I have. I knew you'd change your mind."

She's not in the slightest apologetic, but I don't care. I like her for her enthusiasm and passion for what she believes.

"It needs to be soon. How long do you need?"

She thinks for a moment. "I can have the preparations done by tomorrow evening, but it might not be enough time to get invitations out to everyone. I'd suggest the day after tomorrow, that should give our allies the chance to attend. We really want them here for it to see your power and see the reason why they want to continue to be allied with our Realm."

That's later than I had hoped, but I get her reasoning. In this place, it's all about appearances, and this will be a prime occasion to get all our allies together. I might even be able to combine this with some battle preparation meetings. Multitasking, that's what I'm good at.

"Take whatever resources you need. The treasury is all yours, but please keep the dress simple." I shudder at the thought of yet another dress monstrosity I might be forced to wear.

Tamara chuckles. "Don't worry, it'll be spectacular."

That's exactly what I'm worried about. For her, spectacular means diamonds and a lot of unnecessary fabric. Or no fabric in all the important places. Neither is a very appealing prospect, but even I understand that I can't get crowned the Winter Queen in a t-shirt and jeans.

Gwain still doesn't look happy with the situation. "Flora is still alive and unharmed," I tell him reassuringly. "I can feel it and I think that once I'm crowned, I'll be able to talk to her."

"What? How?" he asks in confusion.

"Until now, the balance was kept by Summer and Winter, but now that Autumn has appeared, Spring has a bigger role to play. I believe that once all four of us are in position, things are going to start moving. The game hasn't begun yet, and I'm sure the Morrigan is aware of that. She's waiting for the final player to take her place. Well, I'm not going to disappoint her. I now know things she doesn't."

I smile, unwilling to tell them anymore. The fewer people know, the better.

"I better go and tell my men that they're going to be Royal consorts soon."

Chapter Nine

My father is fast asleep and my mother is too weak to even respond, which means that neither of my remaining parents can give me some sympathy for my impending coronation. I'm drowning in self-pity and I need an outlet for that.

The guys will probably try and be comforting, but they've all tried to persuade me to become Queen since the issue was first raised. Same with Tamara. Who else do I have to talk to? Ada perhaps? No, I should leave her to recover and spend some time with her men. That leaves only one person... ehm... unicorn.

I focus on my magic and let her run free. She purrs in happiness, jumping all around me, making the books on the shelves around me shake. I've not had the chance to use proper magic recently. Teleporting is different, and the bit of wind magic I did in the Dragon Realm didn't even dent the surface of my powers. *Find Blaze*, I tell her, confident that my magic will find a being more magical than anything else in the Palace.

I mean, the unicorn *eats* magic. It doesn't get more extreme than that.

She runs away and the further she goes, the more my awareness increases. I can hear people talk several corridors away, I can smell the sweat of some soldiers training outside, and I feel the breeze in the courtyard where Blaze is currently snoozing. Wow. I need to do this more often. If I wanted, I could probably eavesdrop on people on the other side of the Palace. No wonder my mother always knows everything.

My magic gallops around Blaze and I zone in on her energy, teleporting to her location a second later. Life is so easy when you're powerful. Too easy. I'm starting to be worried that I might become complacent soon.

"Hi Blaze," I greet the unicorn who's lying beneath a snow-covered tree. He lazily opens one eye.

"Good morning, my lady. Are you here for sparklies?" He grins widely and I smile at him.

"Nope, never again. Storm would kill me if I took any. I assume you haven't heard the way I behaved after your little incident yesterday?"

He flutters his eyelashes at me. "Not a word. Although you should know, unicorn babies are born without horns."

"Blaze!"

He cackles. "Don't worry, Princess, my lips are sealed. But if you're ever interested in how unicorn foals are made, you know where to find me."

"Are you propositioning me?" I ask, stunned.

"No, I'm offering you a science lesson. I'm not into humanoids."

"Thank the Gods."

He grins and gets up on all fours, shaking his shimmering mane.

"Now, why have you come, if not to get sparklies and talk about foals?"

I take a deep breath, before blurting out, "I'm becoming Queen."

He doesn't react surprised at all. "Was there ever any question about that?"

"Yes! My mother is still alive and usually, one Queen has to die before another is crowned."

"Technicalities," he says dismissively. "You've got the makings of a great Queen, and that's what counts."

"Thanks, I think," I mutter, a bit disappointed that I won't be able to get any commiseration from him either. I wish my mum was here. I could do with a hug and some whispered words of confidence and comfort. But no, the Morrigan has taken her away from me. I'll never be able to snuggle against her again. She'll never be able to hold me ever, ever again. The gravity of it all slams down on my heart. I've grieved, but there is still so much sadness deep within me. It hurts.

"Sparklies?" Blaze whispers, but I glare at him and step away.

"Don't tempt me. Please, don't."

He nods. "Sorry, bad joke. Do you want to talk? Is that what humans do?"

"I guess they do, but there's not much to talk about. My mum's dead, my mother is so weak she couldn't even talk to me today, and my dad is traumatised. Everybody wants me to be Queen, but all I want is time to deal with what's happened and spend time with my men. I just want some peace and quiet, Blaze."

He's quiet for a moment, watching me through his dark, beautiful eyes. Then he says, "Touch my horn, Princess."

"No way!" I protest. I have no intentions of blubbering nonsense about baby unicorns again, or worse.

"It's not for sparklies," he explains. "I want to give you that moment of peace that you're craving. No side effects, I promise, and there won't be any time passing here while you're gone. Special unicorn magic."

He gives me a wink. Do I trust him? Well, that's the wrong question. I trust him to be on my side and not to kill me. Do I trust him not to mess with my head and turn me into a lunatic for his own amusement? I'm not so sure about that.

"I promise," he repeats. "It's nothing bad. You helped me, now this is me helping you in return."

"No sparklies?" I ask one last time and he shakes his head with a smile.

"Definitely no sparklies."

"Okay then... but if you're lying about this, I'm going to make you a very, very dead unicorn. I'm sure a unicorn pelt would look lovely on my office floor."

He winces. "I'm about to retract my offer."

Before he can do that, I touch his horn and am whisked away from the courtyard and through the magnificent light of a sparkling rainbow.

I know this place. There's no mistaking the familiar rock formation on the pristine white beach. I've been here many times on family holidays. Barra, one of the islands of the Outer Hebrides, an island where the plane lands on the beach. I used to love that as a child. Oh, who am I kidding, I loved it as an adult too. That moment when the plane wheels hit the ground and sand is thrown into the air, hiding the tiny little airport from view. We got stranded there twice because the plane couldn't take off due to high winds. It's a beautiful place, but why am I here?

"To relax!"

Blaze's booming voice is all around me, reverberating through my bones.

Okay then. He wants me to relax.

"How long do I have?" I shout, not knowing whether he'll be able to hear me.

"As long as you want. Time doesn't flow in this place, so don't feel like you're missing out on things. Just relax and shout when you want to return."

"Ehm, Blaze?"

"Yes, Princess?"

"Can you see me here?"

He cackles. "No, you're in your own head, silly. I'm just supplying the magic to make it feel real."

Phew. That means I can undress and go for a swim. I don't want the unicorn to see me naked. I know he's not even human and is not interested, but still, I prefer my privacy.

I take off my shoes and roll up my trousers before heading towards the sea. Scotland isn't exactly known for its warm weather and I want to test the temperature first.

The water is warm, bathtub kind of warm. Warmer than a heated swimming pool. Okay, this isn't real, this isn't Scotland. This is paradise.

I strip and run into the water, the sand soft beneath the soles of my feet. The waves lap against my naked body like a gentle massage. This is heavenly.

When the water reaches my neck, I stop, looking out over the water. The sun is high over the horizon, its light reflecting on the waves, throwing patterns of brightness onto my skin. In real life, I'd start to worry about sunburn now, but this isn't real. This is a dream, a beautiful fantasy that I'm going to take full advantage of.

I smile and start to swim, daring the waves to carry me back to the beach.

When I get tired from swimming against the current, I turn onto my back and let myself drift, looking up at the beautiful blue sky, interspersed with drawn-out fluffy clouds.

I've not felt this relaxed in a long time. The sun is driving away all my dark thoughts and memories, leaving only contentment and peacefulness.

This is so much better than sparklies. My emotions here are real, not artificially increased. I'm not hyper, I'm happy.

I think back to all the family holidays we had here on Barra. The laughter, the walks by the beach and the live music in the evenings in one of the local pubs. No wonder Blaze sent me here. This is a safe place that I almost forgot about. I don't think anything negative had ever happened on any of the holidays. No arguments, no sadness. I'd always planned to return here to write my thesis, staying in a self-catering cottage somewhere close to the sea, without the distractions of everyday life.

I laugh. My thesis. That isn't going to happen. There are no formal qualifications needed to be Queen. People in the Realms probably don't even know what a PhD is. They don't have schools there, because there aren't any children. There are no universities for the adults either. Guardians are created with all the knowledge and skills they need, and anything else is taught in training sessions. I guess there's the Palace Library as well for all those Guardians who want to learn more. It's strange how I always thought education was essential, but here in the Realms, that's not the case at all.

"Princess?" Blaze calls from all around me. I turn back onto my front and look around, making sure there isn't a unicorn waiting for me on the beach.

"Yes?"

"I have four gentlemen here who would love to join you. Shall I let them in?"

A grin spreads on my face. My Guardians. Did Blaze tell them where I am? Well, it doesn't matter.

"Of course!" I shout back. As beautiful as this beach is, it's much better to share its beauty with others.

A splash to my right makes me shriek in surprise. Blaze seems to have thrown my Guardians into the water rather than let them appear on the beach.

"I'm going to kill that unicorn!" Storm splutters and I turn to him. He's still wearing his uniform, except that it's now drenched and clinging to his body. He's tall enough to stand, but he doesn't look happy about it.

I splash some water at him. "Come on, enjoy it! It's so nice and warm!"

He looks up at the sky and glares at the clouds.

"He got me all wet," Storm complains. "Why can't he just behave?"

I laugh. "Now that would be boring. I can't imagine him following the rules."

Storm looks back at me, smiling. "No, neither can I."

That's when I notice that I can see his smile. His mouth, his nose, his eyes. I can *see* him! The annoying aura has disappeared, letting me see him just like I used to be able to.

Another splash, this time from behind me, and an angry Arc starts shouting curses at a certain unicorn. Storm and I exchange a look and both burst into laughter.

He's actually laughing, properly laughing. Okay, this really is a strange place. My Storm, laughing like a normal human being... well, Guardian.

Frost is the next to arrive, but instead of complaining, he's whooping in joy.

"I love it!" he shouts and starts swimming towards me. "This place is beautiful!"

Arc and Storm look around as if they haven't really noticed their surroundings yet.

"Aye, it's stunning," Arc agrees. "But the water is a wee bit warm."

"You're so Scottish," I laugh. "Most people would be happy to have warm rather than freezing sea water."

He shrugs. "I'm used ta cool air around my legs."

And around other things, I want to say, but his grin says it all. He knows exactly what I'm thinking.

"Why are you all in the water?" Crispin suddenly shouts, making us all turn to look at the beach. He's standing there, hands in pockets, still fully dressed and compared to the others, very dry. We can't have that.

I throw a wind lasso around him and drag him into the sea. He screams as he's pulled into the water while the men around me are roaring with laughter.

"What did you do that for?" he groans when he resurfaces in front of me. "I was very happy on dry land."

"A little too happy, Crisp," Frost chuckles. "If Wyn hadn't pulled you in, I would have."

Crispin glares at him but then turns to me. "So, what are we doing here? Is there a reason we're all standing in the sea with our clothes on?" That's when he realises that I'm not wearing anything. "Oh."

"The elephant in the room..." Arc mutters. "Or the Goddess in the water."

Heat flares through my body. Did Blaze plan this? Whether he did or not, this is a beautiful present. In the real world, we've not had time to be together in ages, not all four of us. Here, time stands still and we can take as long as we want. We can relax together.

The guys are standing in a circle around me, watching me, but nobody's making the first move.

"Do you need instructions?" I ask teasingly. To emphasise my point, I make my magic remove their clothes. There, now we're all naked.

"Did you just undress us?" Storm asks in a deep voice full of promises and sin.

I shrug. "You were too slow."

"Are ye in a rush?" Arc comes at me from behind, little waves signalling his approach. He wraps his arms around my waist and pulls me against his chest. "We can do this fast, if you want."

His cock is pressed against my back, already hard and ready. Do I want this the quick way? Yes, I'm not in the mood for a drawn-out foreplay. I want them, now. But they can take their time once we've started. I don't want this little piece of paradise to end just yet.

Chapter Ten

Arc carries me out of the water and onto the sandy beach, despite my protests that I can walk on my own, thank you very much. The sand has been warmed by the sun and makes a cosy mattress that Arc now lies me on.

"Yer so beautiful," he mutters, looking down at me. I'm the only one on the ground; the men are all standing over me, watching, staring, admiring. It's a bit too much attention.

I stretch out my arms as if to pull the guys down to my level. Frost smiles and kneels at my feed.

"Spread your legs, Princess," he whispers and I do so without thinking. I rest my head on the sand, my breath ragged already in anticipation of what's to come. I'm going to enjoy this, that much is for sure.

Frost's lips graze my thigh, his tongue sliding over my skin ever so softly. It's a touch not much more than a breath, but it makes me shiver in delight. He presses tiny kisses on my thigh, working his way upwards. Electricity is running through my veins, telling my body to prepare for the coming onslaught of emotions and pleasure.

Frost wraps his hands around my thighs and pushes my legs open even further. His lips have almost reached my centre, only an inch or so away. He's so close to making me come apart already. Only a tiny bit more... his mouth is on me, his tongue flicking against the most sensitive spot of my body and I spread my arms, gripping the sand as if to keep me in place. His touch is too much and not enough at the same time. I close my eyes, unable to focus on anything but the feeling of Frost suckling on me. On the spots where his hands are touching me, little lightning bolts are shot into my skin, giving me goosebumps. Then his hands are on my breasts, no, they can't be his, they must be one of the other's. Gently massaging my boobs, then, fingers twirling my nipples, while yet another pair of hands stroking back my hair. Lips on mine, soft yet hard enough to make me open my mouth and let him in. My right hand is lifted from the ground and put around a warm, hard cock. I smile against the kiss. One of my guys is wanting some attention. I start stroking him in the rhythm Frost is setting with his expertly flicks and swirls of his tongue. I'm so close, not much further. So many sensations, it's hard to keep track of them all. When Frost's lips disappear, I want to protest, but I'm busy kissing, and anyway, a moment later something presses against my entrance. Well, I know exactly what it is. I lift my hips to give him easier access, but he doesn't need it, he's gliding into me already. I moan against the kiss, squeezing the cock in my hand a little harder than I probably should. He groans - it's Arc, I think - but then holds my wrist and makes me rub him even faster. Someone begins to nibble on my nipples, a warm mouth holding them captive.

It's too much. I scream and arch my back, coming hard on whoever is fucking me. Sparks are dancing in front of my eyes, rainbow coloured and very sparkly, proving once again that this isn't quite real. Who cares, what I'm feeling is very, very real. I wrap my legs around the man who's still pushing into me, his cock filling me up completely. I'm not going to let him go. I'm not going to let any of them go.

"Wyn, could you remove the ropes from us?" Crispin asks in a pained voice and I can't help but open my eyes. All four of them - including Storm, who I've got inside of me - are having ropes wrapped around their wrists and torsos, making them unable to move much.

I laugh, unable to believe that my magic actually did that.

"Please?"

I'm choking, their affronted expressions making me giggle uncontrollably. I have to say, those ropes suit them. My men. Mine. Definitely mine. Nobody else is allowed to have them, and they're not allowed to leave. Am I turning a little dominant just now?

Storm steps back and I'm suddenly empty.

"Come back!" I command, but he just grins.

"Remove the ropes first."

I know that they could all do it themselves, they're not exactly magicless, but they want me to do it.

"I don't like being blackmailed," I complain. "And I quite like that look on you."

Crispin groans. "We've created a monster."

"I prefer sexually liberated woman," I retort. "But that doesn't mean you can't be *liberated* either."

I tell my magic to remove the ropes and she does as I've asked. Pity. I'd almost hoped I could use my rebellious magic as an excuse.

"Thank the Gods," Frost exclaims and rubs his wrists. "That was uncomfortable."

I smile. "Sorry?"

He winks at me. "My turn."

He pushes his brother out of the way and takes his place between my legs. "No, let's do this differently," he says and sits on the ground instead. "Sit on me, sweetheart."

I don't really want to move, but the sight of his erect cock is enough to make me get up and approach him. I slowly lower myself onto his hardness until I can kneel on the ground, my legs pressed against Frost's hips.

He lifts his pelvis and presses further into me and yet again, I can't prevent a moan escape me. He increases his pace, holding my boobs so they don't whip up and down. He's so deep within me, getting deeper still, that I feel like we're merging, becoming one and the same.

A hand falls onto my lower back, pressing me forward.

"Ready for two of us?" Arc whispers into my ear, his finger already circling the entrance to a place I usually don't think about a lot. Before I met the guys, I never thought I would ever have sex with two men at the same time, but they've certainly changed that feeling.

Arc gently enters me with his finger, rubbing against Frost's cock through my inner walls. It feels dirty and amazing and I need more.

"More," I groan, followed by chuckles from both of them.

"So demanding," Arc mutters, removing his finger and replacing it with his cock. It hurts a little when he enters me, but a bit of healing magic immediately removes that feeling. All I want is the pleasure, the sensation of being close to them. They move inside of me, finding a rhythm that works for both of them. I can no longer keep myself upright and let myself lie down on Frost's chest, my nipples hard against his skin. What are the other two Guardians doing? Why aren't they here?

Frost lifts his head and captures my lips with his, and immediately, all thoughts of the others disappear. He's the best kisser of them all, at least right now, while I don't have anyone else to compare him too. He tastes of sea salt and the freshness of morning dew. I meet his tongue with mine and we begin that most ancient dance, one we have practised before.

Arc grabs my hips and is starting to breathe heavily as he increases his pace. He's close, and so am I. Frost too, I think. Wouldn't it be nice if... I have a crazy idea. And before I can think about it properly, my magic takes it into her own hands.

My four men groan at the same time and I do a slightly more moany sound as the orgasm rushes over all of us. All five of us. Coming together. I ride the wave, dimly aware of how the two men are still moving within me.

"What the fuck was that?" Storm asks breathlessly. "I wasn't... I didn't..."

"Wyn?" Crispin sounds both amused and shocked. "Was that you?"

I keep my eyes closed, feigning innocence.

"I'm not sure I liked that... or maybe I did..."

It seems I've managed to make them all speechless. Arc steps back and Frost rolls me off him until I'm back on the sand. I moan in frustration.

"Just giving you some space," Frost whispers before he gets up.

I sit up, watching as three of them walk away, still naked, their skin flushed, leaving only Crispin behind. I smile, my heart aching at their thoughtfulness. He prefers to be with me on our own, without the others, and that's what they're enabling us to do now.

I pat the sand on my left, inviting him to join me on the warm ground.

He lies down on his back and wraps an arm around my shoulders, letting me use him as my pillow.

"Are you okay with this?" he asks quietly. "I know you like to be with the others."

I turn my head so I can look him in the eyes.

"I like to be with the others, and I like to be with you. Don't ever doubt that you don't count just as much as them."

He sighs. "I want to, but I... it reminds me of..." His voice is shaking all of a sudden. I can't help but turn onto my side and hug him.

"The Morrigan used to... not just me..."

I run my hands over his back, trying to hold back the sadness that is threatening to take a hold on both of us.

"Shhhh," I whisper. "I know. You don't have to say it."

"Sometimes the memories get too much. I try to be strong, but they slip through the cracks and right into the scars she's left on me."

"I understand. I've seen what you've gone through," I say soothingly, pressing him closer to my body. I want him to feel safe. Happy. I want to dispel the demons of his past, but I don't know how. We've made progress, but I'm not sure they'll ever let him go.

"I don't know how I even deserve you," he mutters. "You should run away screaming. You've already got three men, all of them so much stronger than I am, so why do you need me?" His voice has turned bitter.

"Because you're you," I tell him. "And I think you're the strongest of them all. Look at you, how far you've come. You could have just given in and stayed the Morrigan's slave, but no, you fought, and you're still fighting, every day, even now. You're the strongest person I know, Crispy, and I will tell you that as often as you need to hear it."

I run one hand through his hair, playing with his golden locks. "Now relax. Just be with me, in this moment, before we have to go back. I want to look at you, see your eyes, your face. Let's pretend everything is alright."

"We'll find a way to fix your vision," he promises quietly. "There must be a remedy somewhere out there, and I'm going to find it for you."

"Maybe once we've defeated Angus and the Morrigan, my mother will be strong enough to help me." I know that's wishful thinking, but sometimes, the hope of the impossible is all that gets us through times of darkness. In my heart, I still believe that she'll get better, even though my brain tells me otherwise.

"Maybe."

He returns my hug and lets me snuggle against his naked body. The sun is warming our skin, seagulls are calling in the distance, and I am so happy that my heart could burst.

"Crispin?" I whisper. "Thank you for being here with me."

"Any time. Maybe Blaze can show you how to do this trick. We need more moments like this."

"Agreed. Now kiss me."

He lifts himself on his elbows and smiles down at me.

"With pleasure."

Chapter Eleven

"Are you going to marry them?"

Blaze greets us a with a wide grin when we wake up lying on the ground beneath him. All four of my men are by my side, all of them looking rather sleepy.

"What?"

Did I miss part of a conversation?

Blaze sighs. "I thought you may have used the chance to propose to them. A coronation goes so well with a wedding."

I'm speechless, utterly speechless. Who does the unicorn think he is? And me proposing to them rather them to me... well, I guess it makes sense. I'm about to be Queen, maybe it's the etiquette for rulers to propose to their future consorts? But no, I'm twenty-two, I'm not planning to get married any time soon. My plan was always to wait until I'm at least in my mid-twenties, and then maybe think about children when I'm thirty. I have a life to live first.

None of the guys says anything. They're waiting for me to respond. Cowards.

"I think a coronation is enough for now. I don't believe Tamara could handle the stress of adding a wedding to the ceremony."

There you go, I found a reason why it's a terrible idea. And it's definitely not because I secretly want the guys to go on one knee in front of me... no, I'm a strong and emancipated woman. That tradition is so outdated... but I'm also a romantic, and it would be nice... Stop it, Wyn, think with your head, not your ovaries. This is not a time of romance, it's a time of war.

"How much time has passed since we disappeared?" I ask the unicorn.

He sighs again. "You didn't disappear," he explains as if he's talking to a three-year-old. "You were right here, seemingly asleep. But to answer your question, it was mere minutes. Four, five minutes, perhaps? Barely any time at all."

"Good, I have some research to do. Crispin, coming with me?"

He nods and gets up from the ground, shaking the dust off his clothes. For some reason, I'm surprised that we're no longer naked, but of course I shouldn't be. It was all just an illusion.

"We better get back to our duties," Storm grumbles. "I have a meeting with Gwain to discuss strategy. Again."

He doesn't look very happy about it.

"What about you two?" I ask the others.

Arc grimaces. "I need ta find the traitor who gave the clone the password. I have some suspicions, but I need proof before I can tell ya."

"I've got a training session to lead," Frost says, not seeming very enthusiastic. "Some of the fire Guardians aren't very good with defending against water and ice, so I'm going to pretend to be one of the bad guys."

"You are one of the bad guys, little brother," Storm chuckles.

"Little?" Frost roars and begins to fling water balls at his brother.

"Let's leave them to it," I say to Crispin with a laugh and take his hand, teleporting us straight into the library. "I didn't want to get wet, and that looked like the beginnings of a water fight."

"I'm glad I'm working with you today," he chuckles. I wish I could see his smile, but my vision has returned to only giving me the view of their auras, not their faces. "So, what are we doing?"

I turn and look around the library, searching for Algonquin. The Librarian is hopefully going to make this easier by telling me where to find the books I need.

"I'm going to read some books. You're going to make sure I don't go crazy by overdoing it." I smile at him. "I've not experimented enough to know how many books are too many to absorb into my mind."

"Are you sure this is a good idea?" he asks carefully. "Maybe leave the experimenting until after the battle?"

I shake my head. "I wish, but I need this information now, and we don't have the time to actually read all the books. Maybe I've been given this new skill for a reason."

I extend my magic, looking for life signs. There are two Guardians I don't know at the far end of the library, and I find

Algonquin's familiar aura not far from the row of shelves we're standing right now. I take Crispin's hand again and teleport us right in front of the Librarian.

He gasps in shock and I almost regret doing this. He's an old man, and while I'm pretty sure Guardians can't die of a heart attack, I don't want to test that theory.

"Your Majesty." He bows his head.

"Not yet," I mutter, but I don't correct him. I better get used to that title.

"How can I be of service?"

"Do you have any books on the balance of the seasons? Some that mention Spring and Autumn in particular?"

He thinks for a moment. "Not specifically, but there are some chronicles about the struggle of power between Queen Beira and Angus over the millennia. At least two of them refer to Flora, although I'm pretty sure there is no mention of Autumn. Are you aware that there is no God of Autumn?"

I nod. "I know that there wasn't, but there is now."

His aura changes into something that looks to me like enthusiasm. "There's a new God? Who created him?"

"It's a Goddess, and she created herself." I ignore his confused gasp. "That's the next thing I need information about. Are there any books that speak of a union between a female dragon shifter and a God? They had a daughter named Dewi, but I need to know who her father was."

"Not in any of the books we have about the Dragon Realm, but I suppose if the God wasn't from there... let me summon some books that may be relevant."

His aura suddenly flashes bright yellow and books fly towards us from all directions. Now that's a handy trick. I assumed he was going to look at old-fashioned index cards, but of course, I should have known better. This is the biggest library in the Realm, and it's a magical one at that.

About twenty books land in Algonquin's arms and he huffs at their weight, letting them gently float to the floor. "It will take me awhile to find what you're looking for, Your Majesty. What's your priority, the balance of the seasons or the dragon shifter's partner?"

"They're connected," I explain, "and I don't need your help reading them. I can do that myself."

It seems word of my new ability hasn't spread yet. Algonquin will be very jealous once he finds out.

"I'd be happy to help, Your Majesty," he says, sounding like he's a little offended that I don't want his assistance. I better give him something else to do to make up for it and keep him busy.

"That's very kind of you, Algonquin, but I have another task for you. Could you choose some of the best books on battle strategies you can find and send them to Storm, maybe with a written summary? Especially those using guerrilla tactics, please. We might have a new advantage that we can use against our enemies. Oh, and of course anything you might have about dragon wars."

He bows, obviously pleased at having such an important task.

"Of course, milady. I will get on it straight away."

He shuffles off, leaving me with an amused Crispin. "You sure Storm hasn't already read all those books?"

I shrug. "Better safe than sorry. Now, let's read some books. Please make me stop when I go crazy. Or no, scratch that. *Before* I go crazy."

"I think that's enough now."

His gentle voice barely seeps through the words racing across my mind. So many words. Images. Sounds. Pictures. People. Lives. So much chaos. There's no order to them and they make my head hurt.

"Ouch," I say in a whiny voice. "Books hurt."

"Is it your head?"

I nod and immediately regret it. Nodding makes the words bump against my skull and gives me more pain.

Crispin lays his hands on my head and cool air begins to flow into me. Magic, not air. Same thing, isn't?

He begins to massage my scalp, his fingers drawing small circles that feel good. Very good.

"More," I whisper and the coolness increases. The tumbling words slow down a little, but they're still too fast to grasp and understand them. I lean against Crispin, letting myself fall against his chest. He keeps rubbing my head, muttering soothing words to me that are even more complicated than the words in my mind.

"I think it might help if you sleep for a bit," he suggests. It's hard to understand him. His words sound jumbled even though I know they're in the right order. "Just rest, let your mind digest all that new knowledge. Want me to help you sleep?"

"Ouch," I repeat. Such a beautiful little word. So full of meaning.

He gently strokes my cheek.

"Sleep, Wyn. Sweet dreams."

I jump out of bed the second I wake up. So much to do, so much to tell the others.

"Council meeting, now," I say loudly before checking if anybody is actually in the room with me. Luckily, Frost and Crispin are there, playing chess on a small table by the window.

"Glad you're awake, that rescues me from being beaten by Crisp," Frost chuckles and gets up from his chair. "What's up? Why the Council meeting?"

I smile at him. "You know how Blaze said that Summer will be betrayed? Well, I think I know who will betray him. Or better, who has already betrayed him."

I'm giddy with excitement. It all makes sense now. The words in my head have cleared and have assembled in a beautiful pattern. I know so much that will help us. This is the opportunity we've been waiting for.

I run to the guys and touch them on the shoulders before teleporting us into the Council chambers. Nobody's there, but it won't stay that way for long.

"Wait here," I tell them and let my magic search for the Council members. One by one, I appear by their side and teleport them into the room, ignoring their protests. The only one I don't immediately bring back is Zephyr, who's taking a shower. I really didn't want to see that, and luckily, there was a shower curtain hiding him from view. I've told him to hurry up though. The news is waiting to burst from my mouth and I'm not sure how much longer I can wait.

Everybody is staring at me expectantly - at least that's what their auras are telling me - but I wait until Zephyr bursts into the room, his wet grey hair sticking to his forehead. He's put his shirt on the wrong way round, so I ask my magic to correct it. I don't think he even notices, but next to me, Tamara giggles almost inaudibly.

When he's finally sat down, I stand and look at them all.

"I'm not sure how much you already know, so I'm going to start at the beginning. When we went to the Dragon Realm, we met their Queen, Dewi, who said she was a Goddess. Until then, nobody had ever heard of a Dragon Goddess, but Tamara discovered that until recently, Dewi used to be a demigoddess who turned into a Goddess, just like me."

I ignore the frowns and gasps in the room. "According to the book Tamara read, Dewi's parents are a female dragon shifter and a God. Well, the translation must have been slightly wrong, because according to several of the books I read it wasn't a God. It was a Goddess, and we've all heard of her. Any guesses?"

Nobody dares to speculate.

"Bridget. Before she met Angus and became his Queen, she had a relationship with a male dragon shifter. A child is mentioned, but it doesn't reappear until twenty-two years later, when the girl returns from Earth and starts to live in the Dragon Realm. I'm not sure if Dewi was taken away from her mother, or if Bridget didn't want anything to do with her, but I assume the former. Her and Angus have been trying to have a child ever since Beira conceived me, or maybe longer, so I doubt she would have simply given up her baby girl back then."

"But that means...," Gwain begins and I let him follow his train of thought. "Our new ally is the daughter of our enemy?"

"Exactly." I smile. "You've told me that Bridget is whispering in Angus's ear, influencing his decisions. Let's assume she's doing this for power. Imagine if she was to find out that her daughter is now a Goddess and the ruler of the Dragon Realm..."

"She'd want to be on Dewi's side," Storm finishes my sentence. "I don't think she'd go against Angus, but I'm pretty sure she'd try to convince him to change sides. She's a clever woman and if we're lucky, she's begun to doubt whether the Morrigan will let them rule the Summer and the Winter Realms after they win the battle. The assassination of Flora's husband has not just surprised us, but also Angus and his allies, according to our spies. They've seen now that the Morrigan isn't trustworthy and that they're not as safe as they'd thought themselves to be."

"Do you really think Angus and Bridget would change sides?" Zephyr asks sceptically. "No offence, Your Highness, but we've been fighting against them for centuries, millennia in the case of some of us. I doubt they can be swayed this easily."

"The love of a mother," Tamara says quietly, but the room immediately quietens. "There's nothing like it. If Bridget believed her daughter dead, then she'll do anything to keep her alive now."

Gwain turns to me. "It's worth a try. Be aware though that if it doesn't work, they'll know that we have the dragon on our side, and we'll use the element of surprise."

"We still have a few surprises in store," I interject. "I assume Storm has filled you in on the temporary Gates?"

The Master of Arms nods. "Yes, that will be a great tactical advantage. We'd like you to try and teach some of our most powerful mages how to do it. If they can replicate it, we won't be as reliant on the Dragons and on you."

I frown at him. "Are you expecting me to die before the battle?"

The room falls silent and Gwain clears his throat in embarrassment. "No, of course not, Your Highness. I just meant that you might want to stay in the safety of the Palace, and therefore..."

"No way," I interrupt. "I'm going to be fighting alongside everyone else. While my mother is sick, it seems that I am the most powerful person in this Realm. It would be a waste to keep me behind the walls of the capital, you must see that." I'm hoping that appealing to his sense of logic will help. He's a very rational, calculated man.

I decide not to give him any time to argue and turn to Tamara. "I'm sure you have a way of accidentally letting Bridget know about Dewi?"

The spy mistress chuckles. "I do indeed. I'll also work with Ada to make sure that the dragons are prepared in case Bridget tries to contact them."

"Is there any chance of Dewi changing sides if she finds out who her mother is?" Algonquin asks in his old, creaking voice.

"No, not after what the Morrigan did to the Dragon Realm," I say decidedly. "She practically imprisoned every single dragon shifter in their own heads and tortured their Queen. I don't think there's any way they could ever forgive that."

I think of my own reasons for hating the Morrigan. Could I ever work with her if my mother and my friends suddenly switched sides? No, I couldn't. She killed my mum, imprisoned my father, tortured Crispin. There's no forgetting that. And definitely no forgiving either.

I push down the hate bubbling up in me. There's no time to be emotional now.

"Tamara, if you and Ada want a lift to the Dragon Realm, let me know. I need to talk to Dewi tomorrow."

Tamara sighs. "Does that mean I have to reschedule your dress fitting?"

I cluck my tongue in disapproval. "Priorities, Mara, priorities."

Chapter Twelve

I'm going to kill Tamara.

Or the seamstress.

Or both of them.

Now I know why Tamara was sure to ask when exactly I was planning to leave for the Dragon Realm. Not that she would know when to be ready. No, so she could tell the head seamstress to prick and torture me beforehand.

I'm standing on a pedestal in just my underwear and the seamstress is taking great joy in prodding me in all sorts of uncomfortable places. I have no idea why she even needs to measure me. She has magic, for goodness sake. She probably takes great pleasure in pricking the future Queen with fixing pins. I have to keep a close grip on my magic, otherwise the seamstress might have already been set alight.

My first law as Queen will be something about the dress code. Specifically, the Queen can wear whatever she wants, including jeans, t-shirts and baggy hoodies. And if it's a dress, it doesn't need to have frills, a gigantic neckline or holes that show too much skin. All things that I'm dreading my coronation dress to have.

I asked my guys if there are any guidelines for coronations, but it's not something that's ever happened here in this Realm before. Beira was the first and only Queen, there's been no need for a coronation. That's probably why Tamara is so excited. It's a once in a lifetime opportunity, even for immortal Guardians.

There have been coronations in other Realms, however, and Tamara is using those for inspiration. She's even muttered things about William and Kate, but I hope I misheard that. Surely they don't know about Earth monarchies here in the Realms?

"What's the dress going to look like?" I ask the seamstress out of boredom, but she just continues to prick me with needles. That woman has no respect. I have no idea if it's just me she treats in this way, or if she's generally a cold-hearted bitch happy to make other people suffer by making them wear horrible dresses.

To pass the time, I extend my magic and concentrate on the people in the rooms and corridors nearby. Everyone seems to be busy with either war or coronation preparations. I'm beginning to think that they're both just as terrible. There are two people far beneath my room who are talking about the crown. I think the plan is to use my current, smallish Princess crown and turn it into something that resembles that of my mother but isn't quite the same. I refused to wear my mother's crown; I'm keeping that one safe for her until she's better.

I skip a few conversations about the upcoming feast - that only makes me hungry - and stop when I find a group of male

Guardians gossiping over what female Goddesses will be attending the coronation. I smile. Life goes on, even in the middle of a war. I listen to them for a bit, but hurriedly continue on when they start talking about me. No thanks, I have no intention of finding out what the male Palace population thinks about me. It will either make me vain or crush my self-confidence.

A sharp pain on my belly makes me snap back into the room.

"That hurt," I complain, but the seamstress has already turned around and is packing up her things. Good riddance. Maybe I should find out if I can design my own clothes with my new powers. That would be a nice revenge against that mad woman.

I wait until she's left, then I put on some loose linen clothes that aren't suited to the Winter Realm weather in the slightest, but will be perfect for visiting the dragons. I quickly teleport into the kitchen and grab some cinnamon rolls, before heading into my office.

Ada is already waiting there, looking a lot better than when I last saw her.

"How are you?" I greet her warmly while giving her a quick inconspicuous body scan. She's healthy, if still a little underweight. That will hopefully be fixed soon. Her aura is a lot more vibrant as well, swirling with excitement.

"I'm well, thank you. Tamara has told me about Dewi and her mother. Are you sure she's Bridget's daughter?"

"Not one hundred per cent," I admit, "but close. Did she ever mention her parents?"

Ada laughs. "We didn't exactly have time for small talk. I rescued her, she imprisoned me as a thank you, that's the extent of our relationship. But I heard a lot of gossip while I was in my cell. Dewi was a demigoddess before the Morrigan took over, but after I rescued her, something happened and she turned into... more."

I wonder if her transformation happened at the same time as my own. That would be rather interesting. Two demigoddesses, both becoming Gods on the same day. Maybe there's a connection? So far, neither Algonquin nor anybody else has been able to find a record of this happening before. I thought I was unique, but as it turns out, there are at least two of us anomalies.

"Agierth is quite nice though," Ada continues. "She's sensible if a little rash sometimes. She also knows how to handle Dewi's mood swings. The guards said that those were bad before the imprisonment, but have become worse since I freed her. She's not an easy woman to be around." She shrugs. "No idea how Agierth does it."

My magic alerts me that Tamara is approaching the office. I let the door swing open to welcome her in. Much quicker than telling the guards to do it.

"How was your dress fitting?" she asks with a smile in her voice.

"Don't or I can't be held accountable for my actions," I reply tonelessly. "That woman is the devil."

"Oh yes, she likes it when you struggle." She chuckles. "Are we ready for a trip into dragonland? I have to say, I'm rather excited. Their Realm is one of the few places I've never been."

"It's beautiful," Ada says dreamily. "The sunsets are the best, when their dark red earth is bathed in orange light... They have some very strange plants, like small trees with spikes."

"Cacti?" I ask, but she shrugs.

"No idea. We don't have them here, and I've not been bestowed with that knowledge when I was created."

I summon a little fog and form it into the shape of a cactus in front of me.

"Oh yes, that's it!" Ada squeals in delight. "So that's a cacti?"

"Cactus," I correct. "Cacti is plural. But we better get going, I don't want to miss all my coronation preparations."

I'm sure they can hear the sarcasm in my voice. If I could, I'd hide in the Dragon Realm until just before they put a crown on my head. And then go there again to skip the afterparty.

I stretch out an arm and both women put their hands on it.

"Off we go," I warn them and teleport straight into the Dragon Palace.

A roar comes from behind of us and I just about manage to put a barrier into place before a stream of ice crashes into it. What a welcome. Maybe I shouldn't have transported us into the throne room, but I'm short on time.

"Stop, that's the Winter Queen," a shout comes from somewhere in front of us, but with the ice surrounding my barrier, I can't see anything.

The dragon stops trying to turn us into living icicles and I defrost my barrier with a bit of hot air. I check whether the dragon really is halting his attack before slowly lowering it.

"Welcome back," Agierth greets us cheerily. She claps her hands and the room empties as everyone leaves, including the bright green dragon who surprised us.

"Maybe knock the next time you come for a visit," the dragon shifter suggests with a chuckle. "Us dragons don't like being surprised."

Ada steps forward and gives the woman a short bow. "It's good to see you again, Agierth."

"Likewise. I'm glad I no longer have to treat you as a prisoner. So, why have you come?"

"Tamara and Ada will have to talk to you about something important," I tell her. "By the way, may I introduce you to Tamara, my Mistress of the Household."

"A pleasure," Agierth says. If she's surprised that I brought the woman supposedly organising my Palace household, she doesn't show it, not even in her aura.

"I will have to speak to Dewi. Can you point me to her?"

"Not necessary, she's already on her way." Agierth points at her temples. "We're bonded. Does it work the same for non-dragons?"

"It does for me," Ada replies before I have the chance to. "I can talk to my men in my mind when I need to."

I wish I could do the same. Before I became a Goddess, I'd been able to occasionally see their thoughts, but that skill has vanished completely. I can see their auras and I can feel their presence from afar, but I can't do mental communication with them.

"What are you doing here?" Dewi's booming voice makes us all turn around. She's sitting on her throne, even though I'm sure it was empty a second ago.

"I need to talk to you. In private." I'm not sure how pleasant to be to her, not after she imprisoned Ada and her husbands, so I keep my tone neutral.

She looks at me curiously and once again I'm surprised that I can see her face. At least now I know why she's different from other Gods. She wasn't born a Goddess, she turned into one, just like me. Maybe we should be friends or at least swap notes. Well, I've got something like that planned.

"Let's go to my private quarters," she says and walks away without waiting for me to follow. Tamara gives me an encouraging nod, not that I needed it. I'm already hurrying after Dewi.

She leads us through a small door behind the throne and into a cosy sitting room. Thick tapestries cover the wall, all of them depicting dragons. Some of them look ancient and frayed. I wonder how long dragons have been around. Were they created by Gods? Did they spring into existence in another way?

It's a pity I don't have more time. I'd love to spend a few quiet hours in this palace's library and find out more.

Dewi points to one of the sofas for me to take a seat. It's soft and I sink deep into it. Not quite the best way to look royal.

"So, tell me, why are you here?" She's sat down on a chair that looks a little like a throne. It's higher than the sofa, which means that she's looking down at me. Clever. It immediately makes me feel inferior, but I know that isn't true. I'm the future Winter Queen, the daughter of the Mother of Gods.

"There have been some new developments that might change our fortunes in the fight against the Morrigan," I begin, and her gaze turns more focused. She's listening. Good.

"Excuse the personal question, but do you know who your parents are?"

155

She frowns. "I knew my father, but what business of yours is that?"

"I'll explain in a moment. Did he ever tell you who your mother is?"

"No." A look of pain draws over her face. It seems to be a sore point. "I was raised by my father in a dragon commune on Earth. When I was in my mid-twenties, he brought me here. Until then, I didn't even know I was royalty. My father's brother had been the King, and as he'd died, my father took over. I was suddenly a Princess..."

Her voice trails off and I grimace. "I know the feeling."

She looks at me as if she sees me for the first time. "Yes, I suppose you do. We have a lot in common." She pauses, then asks quietly, "So, who's my mother? Even on his deathbed, my father refused to tell me."

His deathbed? Does that mean dragons aren't immortal? A question for another day.

"I believe it was a Goddess. She married later, but back then, she was with your father..."

"Who?" Dewi asks sharply.

"Bridget. The Summer King's wife."

She gasps. "That cannot be. That simply can't be true."

I don't say anything, giving her time for the news to sink in.

"How can you even know that?"

"I found several books mentioning a union between a dragon shifter and a Goddess. One of them mentions Bridget by name. And you being a demigoddess, it makes sense. You're like me, you suddenly became a Goddess."

Dewi smiles. "Yes, it was a bit of a shock. I didn't even know I was a demigoddess before. I always knew I was different from everybody else, that I was a lot more powerful and had skills they didn't possess, but nobody ever told me that I was a demigoddess. I just assumed that it was because I was royalty."

She frowns. "Bridget? Seriously? Angus's wife? Haven't they been together for ages?"

"Strangely enough, no. It's only been a few centuries since they met. How old are you now?"

"Five-hundred-and-twenty-two."

Wow. I still haven't got my head around how old everyone in the Realms is. Centuries, millennia, it's nothing special here. For them, I must seem like a mayfly.

I try not to show my surprise. "That corresponds with what it said in the books. I believe that Bridget has no idea of your existence. She's been trying to have a child, but it's not been successful so far. If she finds out that you exist, she might be tempted to take your side. Our side."

"But she's Angus's wife! She's the enemy!"

"For now." I smile. "I'm hoping we can change that. We're going to leak the news to her, hoping that she'll bite. She'll probably send some spies into your Realm, or even try and come herself. It goes without saying that you should let her. She might even try to keep this a secret from her husband for now, in case he thinks she cheated on him."

"You want me to let our enemy into my Realm?" Dewi asks incredulously.

"I do. And hopefully, by the time she leaves it again, she won't be our enemy any longer."

"Do you really think she can sway Angus to switch sides?"

That's the critical point that I don't have an answer to. Tamara believes so, but I don't know Angus and Bridget. I have no idea what their relationship is like.

"It's worth a try," I hedge. "And wouldn't you like to meet your mother?"

It's a cheap shot, but I don't have time for her to think about it for days. This is war.

Her aura brightens a little. "Of course. Alright, I'll tell my border guards to let in any spies that might come."

"Good." I give her a grateful smile. "Keep me informed if that happens, or if Bridget herself turns up. That would be the best-case scenario, of course. But there's something else. Something about your magic."

"Another surprise?" She smiles weakly. "Was my father not actually my father?"

She's dropped her rough exterior and I can finally see the real Dewi underneath. I think it makes her more human... dragon... Goddess... well, you know what I mean. More approachable, that's it.

"Have you ever wondered why there's no God of Autumn, even though all the other season are represented?"

She shrugs. "I can't say I have. Until recently, we didn't have any Gods in this Realm."

"Neither had I, but now that I'm about to be crowned the Winter Queen, I am more aware of the delicate balance connecting the seasons. Angus and Beira were the first and they've more or less kept the equilibrium ever since. Of course, the God of Summer has tried to take over several times and destroy the balance, but I believe that's just because he's power hungry and not because he actually wants to upset the stability keeping all magic alive."

"Wait, the balance between Summer and Winter is keeping magic alive?"

"Yes, there'd be no magic without it. Not much life, either, if my mother is correct. It's imperative to keep the balance at all cost."

"Then how is there a balance with no Autumn?"

I smile. "I think we already have a Goddess of Autumn, she just doesn't know it yet."

I let the penny drop.

"Me?"

"I think so. There's a way to find out though. Let me connect with your magic. I'm not quite Winter yet, but I will be tomorrow when I'm crowned. I can already feel it though, and I explored the balance yesterday. I learned a lot about it and it gave me some pointers on how we can save it."

"It? You speak as if it's alive."

I shrug. "In a way, that's what it feels like. It's hard to explain. It's like an energy that connects all of us, but it's channelled through the seasons. Without the four Gods, it can't reach the Realms. I just call it the balance, but maybe it has a different name."

"What if I'm not Autumn?"

That question scares me a little. I'm convinced that she is, so if she isn't, what does that mean for my other theories and plans?

I smile bravely. "Let's find out."

She takes a loud breath. "Alright. What do I need to do?"

"Extend your magic until it reaches mine."

I do the same, pushing my magic outwards like a balloon, saturating the air with it. I'm hoping that once it meets with Dewi's, there will be some kind of reaction. Fingers crossed. It's not as if I have any idea of what I'm actually doing. I'm several centuries younger than Dewi, and I'm not sure if my magic is stronger or weaker than hers. It's a strange situation.

I can feel her magic getting closer and prepare for the contact. When they touch, sparks fly. No, not sparks. Snowflakes. It's snowing!

Her magic is warm and intense, but not scolding like I'd imagine Summer's to be. It feels both hot and cold at the same time, like the extremes of an autumn day. The smell of apples and pine needles hits my nose. Yes, she really is Autumn, no doubt about that. She feels like it, like the essence of that season.

"You're Winter," she whispers.

"You're Autumn," I reply. "Look at us, two of the seasons in one room."

"I feel stronger suddenly. Like my magic was suppressed before and now it's finally free."

"Me too," I admit.

"Do you think the same would happen with Angus and whoever the Spring God is?"

"I think so. There's just a tiny problem... the Goddess of Spring, Flora, has been taken by the Morrigan."

Dewi breaks the connection and stares at me. "We need to get her back."

Her voice is full of passion and conviction. Whatever just happened with our magic has changed her. I guess I have always known that I belong to the Winter Realm, but for her, it's all new.

"Trust me, it's on my list. For now, we can't without disrupting the balance. You and I are on one side, and Angus and Flora are on the other, even if she isn't there willingly. What we need to do is get them both onto our side at the same time. If you can convince Bridget to fight with us, and she brings her husband with her, then hopefully together we can free Flora. Imagine, all four of us standing against the Morrigan. We'd be able to stop her, I'm sure of it."

She frowns. "So you don't think we can beat her at the moment?"

"I didn't say that. But it will be more difficult. The losses will be greater. We have no idea how many demons the Morrigan commands. Angus is predictable, she isn't."

"No, that she certainly is not," Dewi mutters. "We had no idea she'd be interested in our Realm. We've been reclusive for so long that we didn't think anyone would ever want to attack us. She managed to take over my Realm without a single drop of blood being spilt." She shudders. "Of course, she caused a lot of bloodshed soon after. She needs to be stopped."

"Don't worry, she will be stopped. She killed my mother, and I'm not letting her get away with that."

Chapter Thirteen

S lowly, the pieces are put into place, ready for their final
moves.

Dewi, waiting for her mother to make an appearance.
Flora, imprisoned somewhere, waiting for our help. Angus,
waiting for the Morrigan's signal to attack. And me, waiting
for my coronation.

Everything has been prepared. The feast, the dress, the crown.
The only thing that isn't ready is me.

"This is a massive mistake," I mutter against Arc's chest. He's
been holding me for the past ten minutes, trying to calm me
down. "I can't be Queen."

"Ye can," he repeats for the umptieth time. "Ye were born ta be
Queen. Doubting that is part of yer strength."

I laugh bitterly. "It doesn't feel like a strength."

"It is. Ye think yer nae worthy, and that's the right way ta
think."

"That doesn't make any sense."

He rubs my back with one hand, the other stroking my hair.

"Believe in yerself, Wyn. It will all be fine."

I wish I had the same confidence in myself that he seems to have. I'm not made to be Queen, but I seem to be the only person who sees that. I'm not strong enough, not clever enough, and definitely not ruthless enough. I pretend to wiggle my way through all the obstacles thrown in my way, but one day, people will see through the pretence. They will see that I'm weak and they'll regret crowning me.

The door opens behind me, but I refuse to look. I don't want this moment to end. Arc is warm and comforting, and even though he's not managed to calm me down completely, it's better than I would be without him.

"They're ready," Storm announces. "Everyone's assembled."

I shudder. No, this isn't happening. This is a nightmare.

"Even Beira is there."

That makes me peek around Arc.

"Beira?"

"She's going to be there for the coronation. She believes in you and she supports you, Wyn."

I step from Arc's hug, regretting it immediately when his warmth disappears from my skin.

"My mother shouldn't be out of bed. She's too weak."

"Then we better get this over with quickly so she can lie down again." Crispin has joined the other Guardians. "But don't worry, she's feeling a lot better today. Maybe it's because the weight on her is being lifted. Now that you're about to be Queen, she can give up some of her responsibilities and focus on her recovery."

I hadn't thought about it like that, but it makes sense. Even though I've been taking on most of her tasks, Beira has still been consulted about matters of state. Hell, I've come to her for help and advice almost every day. I doubt that I'll stop doing that, but still, she'll be under a lot less pressure.

I smoothen my dress and straighten my back. Coronation, here I come.

The Great Hall is filled with far too many people to count. Every inch is packed with visitors, all of them eager to spot a glimpse of their new Queen. Beira is sitting in the front row in a chair covered in blankets. She's pale but Crispin was right, she looks a lot better than she has in the past few days. The throne on the dais is empty, and I'm not going to sit on it just yet. Tamara has gone over the ceremony again and again to make sure that I'll not embarrass myself in front of the crowd.

I refused to walk along the aisle, so instead, I've entered the hall from a door close to the dais. My dress is making it hard to walk and I clutch its skirts, desperately praying that I won't trip. That wouldn't be a good start to my reign, although it would be a fitting one. This is going to be one big stumble after the next.

I take my place in front of the throne – don't sit down, Wyn, don't sit down – and wait for Thor and Lucifer to join me. It took us a while to decide on who should be crowning me, but eventually, we decided on those two. They're both very powerful Gods and good friends of my mother. Hopefully, they're going to be there for me in the future when I need advice and moral support. I suppress a laugh. Having Lucifer for moral support, sure. Not quite what people on Earth would think of him. He's really quite sweet though, especially the fact that he takes human wives and stays true to them until they die, never leaving their side even when they become old.

Loki is here as well, but he's not as strong as his brother, so he's watching from the audience.

Both Gods bow in front of me, then take their place by my side. I wanted my Guardians up here with me as well, but Tamara voted against that. If they were my husbands, then that might have been possible, but as they're not, I need to send out the message that it's me who's ruling and that I'm not being influenced by anyone. I'm the Queen, and while I'm allowed to have romantic partners, it's expected that they don't get involved in politics. I hope they ignore the fact that Storm is part of the Council.

Even Dewi has come, along with several other dragon shifters. Nobody knows yet that she's the Goddess of Autumn, so she's not in the first row along with the other important Gods. We're keeping it a secret for now, not wanting to show our hand to Angus. There's no doubt he has spies here at court.

Gwain appears at the other end of the Great Hall, carrying a crown on a dark blue cushion. He's dressed in his most formal uniform, dozens of medals blazing on his chest. He looks formidable despite his age. Behind him are the other Council members and a few representatives of the military. Most of them look familiar, but I likely wouldn't be able to name them all. They're just there to look pretty, according to Tamara, who'd licked her lips when she said that. She seems partial to a man in uniform, and who could blame her. I look down at my Guardians, all dressed in the uniforms of the Royal Guard. If I could, I'd teleport us all into my chambers and rip off their clothes.

Sadly, I don't think that would go down well with all the assembled dignitaries. Or with Tamara, who's looking at me as if she knows exactly what I'm thinking. She's sitting beside Frost, wearing a dress that looks entirely too modern for someone her age. Well, who am I to judge.

Gwain is slowly making his way towards me. He's far too slow, I don't think I can stand the tension for much longer. There's an orchestra playing in the background, but I can't focus on the music. It could be hard rock or Beethoven, for all I care. My eyes are fixed on the crown. It's a beautiful, intricate design that isn't as heavy as that of my mother, nor as big. It's a bit of a mix between my current Princess crown that's not much more than a diadem, and the current crown of the Winter Queen that resembles rows of upturned icicles. Whoever made it deserves my thanks. It looks like I can actually wear it for several hours at a time, as I will have to do.

"You'll be fine," Thor whispers under his breath. "After the ceremony, you can party and let your hair down."

I don't tell him that I have no intention to do so, because Gwain has finally reached the dais. He stops in front of us and bows, the crown wobbling precariously on its cushion.

"Your Highness," he says quietly, before turning around to the assembled crowd. As one, they all get up. Great, that increases the pressure even more.

He clears his throat before lifting his voice so everyone can hear him. I'm sure there's magic involved to make sure that even those at the very back of the hall know what's going on.

"We have assembled to witness the coronation of Wynter, Daughter of Beira. She has proven that she is worthy of leading our Realm in good times and bad." He turns around again until he's looking at me.

"Is your Majesty willing to take the oath?"

"I am," I reply loud and clear.

Bright, golden magic flares into life, a fiery circle surrounding Gwain, myself and the two Gods flanking me. This magic will assess the truthfulness of my words. I swallow hard. Already, I'm being judged, and I've not even been crowned yet.

"Will you solemnly promise and swear to govern the people of this Realm according to our laws and customs?"

"I solemnly promise to do so," I say, just like I've practised over and over again.

"Will you to your power cause law and justice, in mercy, to be executed in all your judgements?"

I almost cringe at the overly formal language. This is taken directly from the British coronation oath. I think they wanted it to feel familiar, but it's not helping.

"I will."

"Will you preserve the magic that sustains this Realm and our people, and strive to use it for only good?"

"I will."

The magic around us lights up even brighter, before exploding into a thousand tiny stars. They fly up to the ceiling and stay there like a night sky looking down on us. It's beautiful and magical and entirely choreographed by Tamara. I bet she's looking very satisfied with herself just now.

"Then I shall pass this crown on to my superiors so that you may be crowned." Gwain hands the cushion to Lucifer and then retreats, walking backwards for a few steps before bowing and turning.

Finally, I sit down on my throne. The seating area is short, forcing me to sit upright. I can't imagine this being very comfortable for long. No wonder my mother is always cold and impatient when she's sitting on here.

The two Gods take their places behind me. The big moment has come. I'm going to be Queen. I suppress the urge to run and fly far, far away. There's no turning back now. This Realm needs me.

I can feel Thor move closer and I know he's about to hold the crown above my head.

"May this crown be the symbol of our trust in you, our Queen," he says in his booming voice. "May your rule be long and prosper."

Slowly, he lowers the crown until it touches my head. I shiver at the gravity of this moment. When he takes away his hands and the crown sits on my head, pressing against my skin, I take a deep breath. I am Queen.

Queen. Monarch. Ruler.

I'm the Queen of an entire Realm. How did it come to this?

There's applause and shouts, but something is happening. A blackness is covering my vision and I let myself fall back into my chair as I'm ripped from my body and into nothingness.

. . .

"**W**yn?"

A familiar voice is calling to me, but it takes me a moment to place it.

"Flora?"

I open my eyes but there is nothing but darkness around.

"Where are you?" I ask, stretching out my arms in case she's somewhere in the room with me.

"I'm not sure. Everything's dark."

"Hello?" A new voice. It seems Autumn has joined us.

"Dewi?" I call back. "Is that you?"

"Yes. Does anyone want to explain what's going on? I was watching your coronation and suddenly, I'm here."

"I have no idea. Flora?"

"Not a clue either," the Spring Goddess replies. "But I'd rather be here than in the cell they're keeping me in."

"Have they hurt you?" I ask, a little embarrassed that I didn't think to do so right away. "Is it the Morrigan who took you?"

"I'm fine. Nothing that can't be fixed." She sounds resigned. "And yes, it's her. She tricked me. I should have known better, I knew about the Crispin doppelgangers, but I was foolish and well... now she's got me. I've not actually seen her though, and to be honest, I'm glad about that."

"We're going to get you out of there," I promise. "She'll regret this."

"We'll make her regret a lot of things," Dewi adds grimly. "She'll pay for what she's done to our Realms."

"Are my people safe?" Flora asks.

"Yes, nobody has tried to invade," I reassure her. "I've sent some extra troops there just in case."

"Thank you," she whispers and I feel terrible that she's thanking me. I should have protected her better.

Suddenly, someone clears his throat. A man. "As touching as all of this is, could someone please explain what's going on?"

"Angus!" Flora shrieks, confirming my suspicions. "How are you here?"

"Same way you're here. I have no idea what's happened. Good to finally meet you, Winter Princess."

I sneer. "I can't say it's mutual. And that's Queen for you, I just got crowned."

"Ah, yes." He chuckles. "I was going to send flowers, but then decided not to. I'll send some for your funeral instead."

Now that's just rude.

"And who is the other woman?" he asks, but I cut him off.

"None of your business."

"Then I better go, if you're not going to answer my questions."

I wait for him to disappear, but a few seconds later, he protests, "Let me go."

"I'm not keeping you," I explain calmly. "But I think I know why we're here. To talk. To discuss what's going on."

"There's nothing to discuss," Dewi shouts. "I'm not going to talk to an ally of the monster who tried to suppress my people."

"What are you talking about?" Angus snarls back. "Who are you?"

"I am Queen Dewi, the Ruler of the Dragon Realm," she announces haughtily and I suppress a sigh. That was supposed to stay a secret for now.

"Dragons? I have nothing to do with dragons," the Summer King replies, confusion lacing his voice. "I didn't attack your Realm."

"No, but your girlfriend did!" Dewi shouts hysterically.

"My... girlfriend?"

I start to laugh. "She didn't tell you, did she. Oh, she's far too clever to tell her allies all her secrets. Especially not those stupid enough to trust her."

"I'm sure there are reasons," Angus splutters. "Maybe she's hadn't had time to tell me yet."

"She took over my Realm three months ago. I'd say she's had enough time to let you know." Dewi's voice is dripping with poison, but also with a hint of satisfaction. We're at an advantage now. We've planted seeds of doubt in the Summer King's mind, and even though this meeting has come completely unexpected, it's just what we needed. We were planning to have Bridget be the chisel that could divide Angus and the Morrigan, but now we're able to do it from two fronts.

"Sometimes, a true leader has to keep secrets, even from her allies," Angus says, but he doesn't sound as confident and brazen as he did before.

"Maybe ask her what other secrets she's keeping from him?" I suggest lightly. "There might be a few."

"Did you know she was going to kill my husband?" Flora suddenly asks, reminding us that she's here with us as well. "We were your allies, yet you discarded us without a second thought. Is that what she's teaching you? To let go of all alliances and betray the people who trusted you?"

Angus doesn't reply. I bet he didn't know about the assassination before it happened. Yet another seed planted.

"It's not too late to turn your back on her," I tell him urgently. "She doesn't trust you with her plans, what stops her from betraying you? What has she promised you in return for your help? Or is she helping you, using you?"

"We're equal partners," Angus barks out.

He's getting emotional. Good. Now we just need him to think about it, then the doubt will hopefully fester. If only we can get him to change allegiances, then half the battle is already won. Or is that me being too optimistic and hopeful? It's not like I know Angus like all the others do. I'm new to this game of thrones and war, and I don't have any experience I can draw on. I'm hoping that at least this makes me unpredictable.

"I still don't know why we're here," Dewi complains. "I have better things to do than to talk with him."

"Believe me, the feeling is mutual," Angus mutters.

While I'm really glad to have escaped from my coronation for a bit, this is becoming strange. Is it the balance causing this? Are we supposed to do something here? I wish this job came with an instruction manual. 'In case you're abducted and put into a dark room with both friends and enemies, go to step 4B.'

I still don't know where we are. Am I still sitting in the Great Hall and is it only my mind that's been transported here, or have I disappeared from the coronation completely? That would certainly cause some gossip. The newly crowned Queen disappears into thin air the moment the crown touches her head. People would be talking about that for years.

"Is anyone else feeling a little light-headed?" Flora suddenly asks, but before I can answer that I am indeed starting to get dizzy, the darkness disappears, finally letting me see where I am.

Wow. I'm standing in a winter landscape, a forest on the horizon, a few snow-covered shrubs around me. Snow is falling in thick flakes all around me, but it's... wait. It's not falling. It's flying upwards. It's leaving the ground and rising towards the clouds. Exactly the opposite of what should be happening. And why can I see the horizon with so much snow? There's something seriously wrong with this place.

"Hello?" I call, expecting the other Gods to be nearby. We were just talking, they must be close.

"The leaves are turning from brown to green!" Dewi shouts. It sounds as if she's right beside me, but there's no one there. She must be in my head. Does that mean we haven't actually been in the same dark room together? Was it all an illusion?

"The snowdrops are turning into snow." Flora sounds as if she's close to tears, but again, I can hear her as clearly as if she was standing only a few feet away from me.

"What about you, Angus?" I shout, before remembering that I probably don't have to. "I assume you're in a summer world?"

"Everything's burning," he whispers, but it's loud enough for me to hear. "The grass is burning, the trees are burning. It's too hot, the sun is killing it all."

"Is this what could be happening if the balance is disturbed?" I ask into the empty landscape. "Could the world turn into this?"

Most of the snow around me has lifted into the air, and still the snowflakes are rising. What's going to happen next? Will there be more snow? Will everything thaw?

"That balance is a myth that your mother likes to draw on whenever I do something she doesn't like," Angus says angrily. Funny how he describes trying to invade her Realm as something 'she doesn't like'. I'd have some much stronger words for that, but I doubt the Summer God is going to want to hear them.

Dewi shrieks in alarm and I turn in the direction of the scream, but of course, there's nothing to see. We're all both separate and together. Yet another metaphor?

"It's... everything's turning into mud!" she screams. "The leaves, they're falling, but before they touch the ground, they turn into sludge. The trees are melting... get me out of here!"

Flora starts screaming as well, and Angus begins to curse.

"Angus!" I shout. "Do you see what's going to happen if we don't keep the balance? This is a warning, a vision of what's to come. We need to work together to stop this from happening, please!"

He doesn't reply, only curses more. What's happening wherever he is?

"I'm ready to talk and negotiate," I tell him urgently. "If we join forces, we can beat the Morrigan and then fix what's been broken. Please, Angus, listen to reason!"

There's a noise behind me, a roaring sound, and I swirl around. Two tornados are coming towards me, one filled with snow, one made from pure, burning flames. They're destroying everything in their path.

I need to get out of here.

And I am. As soon as I think that thought, I'm back in the Great Hall, the crown weighing heavily on my head. Nobody is staring at me any more than they did before. It seems it was all in my head.

Kind of. Dewi meets my eyes and nods slightly. Yes, she saw it too.

It was very, very real.

Chapter Fourteen

As soon as everyone has started mingling - the benches have magically disappeared to make space for dancing - I turn to my guys and tell them all that's just happened to me.

"Do ye think Angus will change his mind?" Arc asks, clearly very doubtful about that prospect.

"Maybe not because of this vision, but in combination with his wife's desire to be with her daughter... it might be enough to sway him. I'm not trying to make him my best friend, just to stop him from being my enemy."

"Hopefully we'll hear good news from the Dragon Realm soon," Storm says. "I think your mother would like to talk to you."

I turn and follow his gaze. Beira is still sitting on her chair, but she looks paler than she did at the start of the ceremony. Time to get her back into bed.

"I'll take care of her. Guys, could you mingle a bit? I'd quite like to know what the other Gods think about me being Queen now."

Crispin sighs. "As long as I don't need to flirt. I hate flirting."

I frown. "I'm having trouble believing that."

He chuckles. "Flirting with you is amazing. Flirting with other women is annoying. They get all flustered and blush and giggle. I can't stand giggling."

I grin and leave them to it, heading to my mother.

"Beira." I bow my head to show her that I still think her far above me, despite me being Queen now. She's never officially abdicated, but so far, nobody has questioned that. Maybe people will accept two Queens, or maybe they just have too many other things to worry about just now. War is a little more important than how many thrones there are.

"I'm so proud of you," she says, her voice so quiet I'm having trouble understanding her. "You did very well."

I shift the crown on my head to a better position. I should start taking bets on how long it'll take for me to drop it. Or lose it, in the worst case scenario.

"How long did it take you to get used to the crown?" I ask and she smiles weakly.

"I was wearing the crown when I first opened my eyes. It's part of me, and don't worry, it will become part of you too. It takes time to get used to the role, but I'll be here whenever you need advice." She clears her throat, another weak, aching sound. "Could you help me back to my chambers?"

I nod and gently take her arm, teleporting us straight into her bedroom. I help her into her bed and make sure the pillows are supporting her back. She looks exhausted, but I can't leave without asking her a question.

"During the coronation, when the crown was first put on me, I had a... I'm not sure what to call it... a vision. I talked to Angus, Dewi and Flora, and then we were each in a landscape matching our season. It was winter for me but the snow wasn't falling, it was rising upwards. Has this ever happened to you?"

She looks at me with curiosity. "No, I can't say it has. I am able to talk to Angus telepathically, but it means opening myself to him, which is something I try to avoid. We've done it in times of peace when we had to speak to each other urgently, but I've not talked to him in that way for decades. It's curious that it happened to you now, but it also makes sense. The four Gods have taken their places, but with four rather than just two, it will be even harder to maintain the balance. All four of you will have to work together."

She sinks back, exhausted from her long speech.

"Let's hope Angus realises that," I mutter. "I'll let you rest for a while. Do you need anything?"

Beira smiles. "No, but please try and enjoy the celebrations. Bad times are coming, so you ought to enjoy the happy moments while they last."

I really hadn't planned to join the party, but Beira's advice makes sense. This is the calm before the storm and who knows when we'll have time to celebrate again.

I teleport back into the Great Hall and search for Dewi, but she seems to have left already. The guys are mingling as I asked them to, but Crispin's aura is flashing with annoyance as five female Guardians are surrounding him. I'll need to rescue him soon.

Before I can reach him, a familiar God steps in my way. Thor. His aura is radiant, but it lets me see his face, like with most Gods. The stronger the God, the more I can see their expression.

"Your Majesty." He bows and smiles at me. "Congratulations, this was a most exciting coronation."

"I'm glad you enjoyed it," I say tonelessly, hoping he won't notice my lack of enthusiasm. "Are you going to stay for the celebrations?"

He grins. "Oh yes, I wouldn't miss it for the Realms. Life has been far too serious recently, and we can all do with some fun times."

That's almost exactly what my mother said, and most guests seem to think the same. The dancing is wild and boisterous, and the atmosphere is so relaxed it's almost too much so. Looking at the half-naked Guardians surrounding some of the Gods, I'm worried this might turn into an orgy soon.

"Have fun then," I tell him with a grin. I know he's married and has a daughter, so he might stay away from the naked Guardians, but I'm sure he's going to partake in all the other physical pleasures that will be offered this evening. Tamara has chosen some of the best wines from our cellar, including some from other Realms. The tables on both sides of the hall are overflowing with food and snacks, and I'm drawn to the chocolate fountain that's appeared close to the main doors.

"I need to tell you something," he says, still smiling, but his eyes are flickering over the people surrounding us as if to make sure nobody is listening in. "Dance with me."

Without waiting for a reply, he wraps an arm around my waist, takes my hand and begins to waltz. I follow his lead, hoping I won't step on the toes of the God of Thunder. That would be embarrassing. The crown on my head feels like it's going to slip, but Thor is holding me tight. He lowers his head until he's a little too close for comfort.

"There's a spy in this room," he whispers into my ear.

"I'm sure there's several," I whisper back, not surprised at all. From the beginning, Tamara was always very clear that there are several agents of our enemies living in the Palace. Sometimes, she feeds them the wrong information, and sometimes, she lets them pass on real nuggets of truth to make sure they maintain the trust of their masters.

"Yes, but not all of them have let in an assassin." I lean back to look at Thor, but he keeps his grip on me. "Don't look. There are two Crispins in this room. One talking to some women, the other is whispering to a man I don't know. They probably didn't expect a God with excellent hearing to be present. I'll turn us in a moment so you can take a look."

My heart sinks. Not another Crispin clone. This is getting old, and having him and the real Crispin in the same room is a little obvious. Is the Morrigan this desperate? She must be aware that we all know of the Crispin clones and that all Palace staff have been warned. There are passwords that change daily... not that it prevented Flora's abduction.

Thor swirls me around in an elegant move. He really is an excellent dancer. If I was into dancing, I'd ask him to give my men some lessons, but I'm not. My hand-foot-coordination just isn't up to scratch.

"In the corner, by the dried fruit stands," Thor whispers. It takes me a moment to spy fake Crispin's blond hair in the crowd. When I recognise the man he's talking to, I'm not really surprised. I should have suspected this.

"That's Magnus, our former treasurer," I explain. "I relieved him of his duties not long ago. He's always been strange, but I thought that if my mother trusted him, I should too."

"The older us Gods are, the blinder we can be to those around us," Thor says sagely. "Sometimes it's staring us right in the face, but we no longer pay attention to the obvious. Magnus wants you removed, and the impostor said he'd be happy to oblige."

Magnus's betrayal is no surprise, but it still leaves a bad taste in my mouth. I'd hoped he just didn't like me, but he actually seems to hate me enough to let an assassin into the Palace. I'm sure it was him who helped with Flora's abduction, too.

"We need to separate them," I whisper. "I'll let my Guardians know and then I'll pretend I don't know he's not the real Crispin. Can you draw away Magnus?"

Thor nods. "I'll think of something. Where do you want me to take him?"

I grin. "Do you know where the dungeons are?"

His cheeky smile is all the answer I need.

We end our dance and I look for my closest Guardian. Storm is leaning against a column, looking bored and grumpy. Good, he'll be grateful for the distraction.

I join him and casually wrap an arm around his waist.

"Pretend you're kissing me," I mutter under my breath.

"I don't need to pretend," he replies and the intensity of his voice makes my ovaries jump in excitement. Down, girls. Not now. I have work to do.

He leans down until his mouth almost touches mine. His lips are hovering close to my skin and I can feel his hot breath.

"Magnus is talking to a clone Crispin," I say hurriedly before I'm tempted to kiss him and forget all about the potential assassin. "Thor is going to lure Magnus away, and I'll take care of fake Crisp. Can you keep the real Crispin away? I want it to seem like I don't realise he's a clone."

"You shouldn't be doing this alone," Storm protests but I put a finger on his lips to shut him up. He opens his mouth and sucks on it. Well, there goes that idea. Tingling spreads through my hand and I really want to take this further, but I'm the Queen now. I need to look after my subjects.

Look at me, using proper language like subjects. Soon I'll be talking about taxes and other horrifically boring stuff.

"Keep Crispin away," I repeat. "If you must, you can follow me after, but don't worry, I can handle this on my own. I'm stronger now than the last time and I have the aspect of surprise on my side. Let's just try and keep this under wraps, I don't want our allies to think that we're weak by letting assassins enter our Palace."

He nods, but his aura is darkening. He doesn't like me doing this. Well, he'll have to get used to it. I'm the bloody Queen of this bloody Realm and I can make my own decisions. I swallow my anger; it's not him I should be angry at. It's Magnus and the clone. They're ruining my coronation.

I leave Storm to look for the real Crispin and head to the corner where I last saw the two men I'm looking for. Magnus has disappeared, hopefully called away by Thor. The clone is still there, nibbling on some dried fruit. He seems to enjoy himself. That's going to change in a moment.

I smooth my expression and approach him from behind.

"There you are! I've been looking for you!"

I should probably hug him to make it more convincing, but I can't bring myself to do it. This is an impostor, someone the Morrigan created and trained. He might try and kill me any moment, although if he's clever, he's going to wait until we're alone.

"What's up?" he asks, sounding just like Crispin. I extend my magic just to make sure that he's a clone. Yes, there's none of the familiar bond I have with my Guardians.

"Tamara said she has a surprise," I tell him, "a present for just the two of us. Shall we take a look?"

He looks a little confused. Wait, I can see his face. There's no aura. How did I not notice this before? Crispin's beautiful face. His eyes, his smile, his kissable lips. But no, that's not him. And why doesn't he have an aura? Everyone does, even Gods, even dragon shifters. He's the first person in the Realms who I've seen without one. Very strange. Does that mean he doesn't have magic? Or is it because he's a duplicate, a shadow of someone who's already existing?

"Where's the surprise?" he asks, looking around the room as if he's searching for Tamara. Luckily, my magic has already confirmed that she isn't here. "And why only us? Why not the others?"

He's far too suspicious for my taste. I need him to trust me; I don't want him to be on his guard.

"She said in the magic training courtyard where Blaze likes to be. Maybe it's got something to do with Blaze? You know how secretive unicorns like to be."

"Oh yes." He nods, even though I'm not sure if he's ever met a unicorn before. I really hope he hasn't, because that would probably mean that the Morrigan has one captured. I don't even want to think about that.

"Good, then let's go," I say cheerily and take his hand, pulling him with me.

"You're very excited," he remarks, but he follows me without struggle.

"It's my coronation, of course I'm excited!"

I keep him at my side, so I can see what he's doing. I have no intention of getting stabbed in the back.

"I can't wait to see what she got us," I babble, trying to make myself sound careless and overly happy. I want him to be less tense.

"Yes, neither can I." He doesn't sound enthusiastic at all. "It must be something special if it's just for you and me."

"I'm sure she's put a lot of thought into it." By now, I'm almost expecting Tamara to be in the courtyard, but when we enter it, it's abandoned, just like I'd hoped. Everyone is in the Great Hall to celebrate, and the only rooms that are guarded are the Royal Quarters, which is why I couldn't take him there.

I have no idea where Blaze is. I'd expected him to come to the coronation, but he wasn't there, and he's not here either, in his favourite spot. Maybe he's left the Palace? He came without warning, could he be gone without saying a word either? No, he loves attention too much for that, he'd probably want us to hold a big farewell ceremony for him.

"There's nobody here," Crispin remarks, his voice turning cold. I think he knows that he's been discovered.

"Maybe she's running late?" I suggest while gripping my magic and wrapping it tightly around me as a barrier. I make it hard, but invisible, an impenetrable armour that will keep him from injuring me physically. My mental barriers are up and strong. He's got no chance of injuring me unless he uses some very powerful magic.

"Or maybe she was never here." He looks me straight in the eyes, the blackness in them so unlike the beautiful warm eyes of the real Crispin.

"Maybe," I agree. "What now?"

"I'm not here to kill you," he says calmly, dropping all pretence. "I've been sent to deliver a message."

"Why were you talking to Magnus?" I ask, ignoring what he just said.

The clone shrugs. "He's my contact here. I was to deliver a message to him as well, but he got called away before I could."

"Liar," I hiss. "Your conversation wasn't as private as you thought. I know you want to kill me."

He laughs coldly. "Want? Yes. Allowed to? Not yet. I just told that old man that to make him trust me."

"Why wouldn't he trust you?"

"Not everyone is able to tell whether I'm real or not. I needed to convince him that I'm the Morrigan's."

"Why are you working for her?" I ask, even though I know that he's likely too far gone to be swayed. "Don't you know what she's doing?"

"She's creating a better world, and once her vision is complete, I'm going to be at her side, looking down on our new creation together."

I laugh and he frowns at me. "Seriously? The Morrigan doesn't do *together*. She'll discard you as soon as you're no longer useful to her, just like she does with all of her allies. She's not interested in anyone but herself."

"You're right about that." The smile slips from my lips. The clone's voice has changed, it's higher now, almost shrill. His face is blank, looking even less like my Crispin. "Hi, sweetie. It's so nice to finally talk to you." He giggles girlishly. "Nice crown. It will go well with my other one."

"Morrigan?" I ask, even though I know it's her. The blackness in his eyes is the same I've seen in Crispin's memories. Somehow, the Morrigan is possessing her creation.

"Just the same." She giggles again and I'm tempted to slap her. What did Crispin say about giggling girls earlier? No wonder he doesn't like it.

"What do you want?" I don't even try not to sound hostile. If I knew I could kill her while she's possessing the clone, I'd do it in a heartbeat. She killed my mum. Sparks are dancing before my eyes as I try to hold back my anger and hate. She's not really here. I can't hurt her. Well, that's what I think at least. To be honest, I have no idea how she's doing this.

"I thought I'd come for a little visit. He did tell you that he was bringing you a message, didn't he?" She grins and looks down at her male body. "He's so handsome. I remember his body, how he felt when he was touching me... So talented, that boy, so very talented."

I shudder in disgust and erase the image of her and Crispin from my mind. He was forced to do it, it wasn't his choice. First, he was brainwashed, then she kept him under control by threatening a baby's life.

"What do you want?" I repeat coldly.

"To send a message. You'll understand in just a moment. I'm glad you got us outside, the view will be so much better from here."

I have no idea what she's talking about.

"Just give me your message and be done with it," I growl, tightening my grip on my magic.

"So impatient," she cackles. "Your mother would be disappointed. Well, she might be, for a few more seconds. Then she won't be able to anymore."

"What?"

"Oh sweetie, you're rather stupid, aren't you?"

She's smiling at me with Crispin's face and it makes me want to throw up. She's planned something bad, and it's about to happen.

The view... I look up. I can see several of the highest towers from here, including that which houses my mother's quarters. Oh no. She's going to attack Beira. What's the point though? My mum's already weakened and I'm now the one in control. Getting me out of the way would make so much more sense. Unless... she's the Morrigan. She likes to make people suffer.

Beira.

I spread my wings and jump into the air, flying towards the tower as fast as I can. Down below, I still hear Crispin's high-pitched laughter. I throw a fireball in his direction and beat my wings even faster. I need to get a better idea of the situation, and I can't get that by teleporting into my mother's quarters. I doubt the Morrigan would be doing something in there where nobody can see. No assassins this time. No poison. She wants everyone to know how we're not safe even in this Palace.

I pull on the bond connecting me to my Guardians, alerting them to danger, then spread out my magic to feel for threats.

Find whatever's endangering my mother, I beg it, hoping that for once, she'll do as I ask. She quickly races through the walls into the tower, exploring the rooms. I send her into my mother's bedroom first. There are no other people in there besides Beira, sleeping in her bed. Maybe there's some kind of magical artefact hidden in her quarters?

My magic finds something and I immediately teleport to where she led me. It's a round orb, floating in the air, pulsating with black, strange light. It's almost as if the light of the room is sucked into it and that's what's making it shine.

"What is that?" I whisper, not expecting an answer.

The pulses begin to become faster and the orb seems to expand slowly. Whatever it is, it can't be good. I wrap some air magic around it and throw it out of the open window, as far away as I can. It fights me, wants to stay, but I'm stronger. I run to the window and look at the orb. It's almost the size of a person now, thick and black and entirely evil. I push it even further away, out of reach of any of the buildings of the Palace.

My magic warns me a fraction of a second before it happens, but it's not enough warning. The orb suddenly explodes and my magic is pushed away from the explosion, slamming back into me, throwing me onto the floor.

"What's going on?" my mother asks weakly, barely managing to lift her head.

"The Morrigan," I answer grimly and jump back to my feet. Outside, a black fire is burning in the air, hovering where the orb was before. I don't want to imagine what would've happened had the sphere still been in this room. It would have been a massive explosion.

Ash is raining down from the sky as the blackness is slowly disintegrating. It could almost be beautiful if I didn't know what almost happened.

She's going to pay for this.

I teleport back into the courtyard, but the Crispin clone is lying on the ground, unmoving. I have my magic check him, but I already know that he's dead. He was wrong and I was right. The Morrigan doesn't do *together*.

M y first Council meeting as Queen comes a lot earlier than planned. After the near attack on my mother's life, I couldn't just go back to the celebrations. I didn't stop them, either, but I had the Council members informed. Now we're all sitting in our usual meeting room, but the mood is even more sombre than it has been in the past weeks.

"How did he die?" I ask Theodore, the healer.

"There are no external injuries, no signs of poisons. It seems his heart stopped without a physical reason."

"Then let's just assume the Morrigan killed him. What I don't understand is why she would warn me in time to prevent the explosion? She could have waited a few minutes. We were outside anyway, we would have seen it even without her telling me in advance."

"Good question," Tamara mutters. "Maybe she wanted to show off? Got a bit overexcited?"

"She may be a psychopath, but every single one of her actions is calculated," Crispin says. I've asked my Guardians to join this Council session and they're sitting by my side at the head of the table. "She wanted you to stop it. Why?"

Nobody answers. How should we know? It doesn't make any sense. This was supposed to be a surprise attack. If Thor hadn't overheard Magnus and the clone, we would likely never have noticed that we had yet another Crispin impostor in the Palace. The orb would have exploded without any of us the wiser. We may have assumed it was Angus rather than the Morrigan.

"If anyone thinks of a reason, let me know," I say tiredly. It's been a long and exhausting day. I'd love to cuddle up with my Guardians now and forget about it all, but no, I can't. I'm the Queen.

"Let's -"

A tremor shakes the room and I jump up, looking around me in alarm. Most of the Council members have done the same, a mix of confusion and fear covering their auras.

"Mum."

I teleport while still saying that word - and excruciating pain races through my body as I'm torn apart.

. . .

S now is surrounding me when I wake. Thick flakes are raining from the sky... no, it's not snow. It smells of burning and death.

Ash.

I want to sit up, but my body isn't moving. I'm broken, hurt inside, the pain only now filtering through my consciousness. So much pain, everywhere.

Tears run down my cheeks and mix with the ash that is falling on my body. It's covering me like a deathly blanket. Soon, I'll be hidden from view, buried under the ashes of my mother. Darkness is teetering on the edges of my vision and I let my eyes fall shut. With one last conscious effort, I pull at my bond, hoping my Guardians will hear me. If they're still alive.

Chapter Fifteen

"I never really wanted to kill her. I just wanted her to be defeated."

"Well, look where that got us. She's dead."

"Wait, I think I can feel Wyn."

Three voices, all familiar. A man, two women.

"Wyn? Are you there?"

That's Flora, sweet, lively Flora. Spring.

"I'm... what's happening?" My thoughts are slow, far too slow to make sense of it all.

"We're back in the dark room. For the third time today, I think. We were here twice yesterday."

"Wait... what..."

I still can't form a coherent thought. Everything is so confusing.

"There was an explosion at your Palace, do you remember that?" Dewi's voice is surprisingly gentle. "That was two days ago. You've been unconscious until now, maybe you still are. I've been getting hourly reports from your assistants, but right now... well, they can't really tell me anything while we're in here."

"Two days?"

It feels wrong. That can't be true. Unconscious for two days? But I'm a Goddess. I should have healed by now.

The man clears his throat. Angus. "I'm so sorry."

"You should be," Dewi seethes, her voice no longer calm at all. "She's your ally."

"Was," he grumbles. "Was."

"Wait, you're no longer...?" At least, I almost manage to ask a proper question this time.

"No. I'm not." He takes a deep, loud breath. "I didn't know she was going to attack Beira. I had no idea. Just like she hadn't told me about Flora and Fav. I'm sure there were many other things she hasn't informed me about."

"You're on our side?" I ask weakly and his assent filters through to me.

"Yes, I am. All four of us are united now. I've shared all I know about the Morrigan's battle plans with Dewi and Flora, although Flora is still a prisoner."

"Not much longer, if I have anything to say about it," Dewi says confidently. "I've got a plan to break you out of there."

I've missed so much. Angus, on our side. Flora about to be rescued.

"Dewi... your mother?"

A wave of happiness streams through the dark room. "We've talked. I know she's my mum, I can feel the connection. She was told I'd died on the way to Earth."

"I hadn't expected to suddenly have a step-daughter," Angus chuckles. "Now we're not only allies, but family."

I'm not sure if I can trust him. He's been the enemy for so long and he's suddenly changed his mind, just like that? Wait, he said something at the beginning. Something dreadful and terrible that I've pushed from my mind.

"What exactly happened?" I ask and silence falls.

"You teleported right into an explosion," Dewi finally says. "You got torn apart. Nobody thought you'd survive, but... ehm... well, it's a bit gruesome, but you grew new limbs. The ones you lost, I mean, not completely new ones. Don't worry, you still have two arms and two legs, except that half of them are brand new. Maybe more than half, more like three quarters."

I shudder, unable to believe what she's saying. It has to be a joke. You don't just grow body parts when you lose them. Not even Gods do that. Until now. Until me.

"I assume it was the Morrigan?"

"Oh yes. The first bomb was to show you what she can do, the second to actually do the deed."

I begin to shiver. "What deed?"

Again, silence.

"I'm so sorry," Flora whispers. "Beira is dead."

I don't want to wake up. The dark room has disappeared and so have the three Gods, but I'm not ready to return to the living. Beira, dead. My mother. Now I've lost both my mums. My father is the last remaining family I have. How am I supposed to function, to fight, with so much sadness in my heart? So much grief. It's filling me, my veins, my bones, not letting me move.

I can't deal with this, I just can't. How much sadness can one heart feel before it dies?

Not that my heart can die. I need to start accepting that I'm immortal now, and even less killable than other Gods. I *grew* a new body. People just don't do that, not even in the Realms.

Beira is dead.

I'm alive.

It's so not fair. She's the Mother of Gods, the very first Goddess of them all. How can she just disappear? It shouldn't be possible. It's wrong.

Did I perhaps contribute to it? Could she have died if I hadn't been crowned? Maybe the universe thought she was no longer needed now that there was a new Queen.

The universe. The balance. The seasons. They can all go screw themselves. I'm done with all the heartbreak. From now on, my life is going to be good. I'm going to kill the Morrigan and her demons, and then I'm going to turn this Realm into a paradise without suffering. Not for me, not for any of my subjects. The Winter Realm is going to be a place of peace, of happiness.

No more war. Just this one, final battle. And I'm done waiting for the battle to come to me. I'm going to bring war to the Morrigan and end her once and for all.

I wake with a grim smile. A body is warming mine. I let my magic explore the room before I open my eyes. Four people. Arc is the one in my bed, holding me close as if he's scared I might disappear. Theodore is sitting in a corner, half asleep. The other two are guards, standing by the door, wide awake and ready to react to any threat.

I don't know this room. It's neither my bedroom nor the infirmary. I push my magic out further. We're underneath the main Palace in an area I haven't explored yet. The walls here are thick and ancient, gleaming with a strange substance that repels my magic. It's possible for me to push through it, but it's not easy. They must have put me in the safest place they could think of. An area where magic is inhibited, so enemies couldn't use it against me while I was defenceless. Clever.

There's a smaller room beside this one, and inside are my other three Guardians. Crispin is sleeping. I'm glad; his aura is faint with exhaustion. Storm is awake, walking up and down, brooding. Frost is sitting by Crispin's side, his aura as restless as that of his brother.

I gently pull on my bond to them and watch as they all jump up and run out of their room and into mine. Storm commands the guards and the healer to leave and they immediately do as he asks.

The arms around me tighten.

"Welcome back," Arc whispers, before loosening his grip and disappearing from my bed. Why is he leaving me alone?

Crispin is the first to approach me. Magic pours from his hands as he examines me for injuries.

"Wyn? Can you hear me?"

"Loud and clear." My voice is surprisingly strong, not as weak as I'd expected. For someone who just regrew her body, I sound pretty good.

"How are you feeling?" His magic is still examining me, but all I can feel is a slight tickling sensation.

I check my body for pain. There's a dull ache in my right arm, but that's about it. I can't imagine I was seriously injured just two days ago.

"Pretty good," I reply. "What's the situation?"

They look at each other. The elephant in the room. No, the dead Goddess in the room.

"I know," I say tonelessly. I can't afford to break down now. "I know she's dead. I also know about the explosion, and that Angus is on our side now. I had a little conference call with the other three season Gods."

"You know about Bridget too, I suppose?" Storm asks.

"That she's Dewi's mother and supporting us? Yes."

"This is weird," Frost mutters. I tend to agree. I'd love to still be sickly in bed and surrounded by my loving, caring Guardians, but there's no time. I can feel the change in the air. The storm is about to come and hit us hard.

"Angus says the Morrigan might not be aware that he's no longer on her side," Storm reports. "She's ordered him to get his troops ready, and he's going to pretend nothing's changed for a while longer. Only his highest generals will be briefed, and that only just before the battle. Hopefully, it will be a surprise to her when Angus's forces suddenly turn and fight the Morrigan's demons."

"Is everyone ready? Our allies?"

Storm nods. "Yes, they're all waiting for the signal. Angus has been trying to stall the Morrigan so you had time to heal. I don't think she's going to wait much longer though. Her demons are no longer staying hidden and they're amassing by the Gates."

"A distraction," I mutter. "She can build her own Gates, remember? She'll create one somewhere in the centre of this Realm and invade while we're watching the existing Gates."

"How do you..." Storm is speechless. Wow, the day I got to see that.

"Something has changed. My mind is different, More open. I can *feel* more."

"I'm nae sure I understand," Arc says, his aura fluttering with uncertainty. "What's changed?"

"My powers. My connection to the magic around me. I'm not sure if it was the coronation or the death of my mother, maybe both. I know things I didn't before. My mind has grown."

Only now that I put it into words do I understand the gravity of the new sensation. I'm even stronger now. I have knowledge, ancient knowledge, that is just waiting to be explored and made use of. Like how the Morrigan has acted in the past. How she thinks. How I created her.

Wait.

I didn't create her.

203

"My mother's memories," I whisper. "I can access some of her memories."

"That's crazy," Frost exclaims, but immediately adds, "and useful."

I try and locate the memories that aren't mine, but they're merged with my own. They have a slightly different taste to them, but it's almost imperceptible. I will need time to sort out what's hers and what's mine. This is going to be confusing as hell.

I think about the Morrigan and new memories appear. I smile at one in particular.

"The Morrigan was created as a warrior. That's how she thinks, in terms of violence and destruction. She also assumes that she's the only one to be like this. She doesn't expect us to take the first move."

"And we didn't plan to do that," Storm says slowly. "Are you saying we should?"

"Nobody knows that I'm awake. Her spies will not have been able to tell her otherwise... yet. She thinks we're weak and she's going to attack soon. Angus might be the only reason why she hasn't yet. We need to be faster than her."

"As soon as we tell our allies, she'll know," Storm points out. "She has spies everywhere."

"Oh yes, she does." I smile. "But she's not in their heads. I can be."

They all stare at me.

"I can feel the Gods in the Palace above," I explain. "I know I can talk to them telepathically. I also feel which ones are on our side. There's at least one who isn't, and two who aren't quite sure."

"Who?" Storm asks immediately, his aura darkening.

I concentrate my magic on the minds that stand out. They're like dark spots standing out amongst all the white, bright minds of the Gods. Guardians are more of a silver hue, and there's one pink dot that makes me smile. Blaze.

"Saturn is a traitor," I tell them. I've not talked to that God in person yet, even though I've seen him around. "Hades is undecided. His sister has persuaded him to join us, but he sees it as a lost cause. He'll turn as soon as he feels himself in danger. The other one I don't know... wait, I do. Aeolus, the God of Wind."

"Aeolus?" Storm asks in bewilderment. "He's been really supportive in the past. He's not very powerful and his Realm is tiny, but I never doubted his commitment."

I shrug. "He's scared. He might just need a little pep talk. Give me a moment."

I concentrate and block out the people surrounding me, focussing on the bright light of the God. He's going to get a bit of a shock.

"Aeolus!" I call in his mind, hoping that my instincts didn't deceive me about my new skills.

He shrieks internally and I have to suppress a smile. He's rather skittish.

"Your... Your Majesty?"

"Indeed. How are your battle preparations going?"

"Good, great, everything is ready." He reminds me of a hamster that's running around in his wheel, scared to jump out of it.

"We will win this fight, Aeolus," I say, showing him my conviction through our connection. "I know it's easy to doubt that we'll be able to win against hordes of demons, but we're strong together. Shall I tell you a secret?"

I assess his mind while talking to him. Will he pass on anything I say to the Morrigan? No, he's just scared, he doesn't actually want to support her. If he bows out, he's just going to crawl back to his own Realm and hope for the best.

"Your Majesty?"

"We have new allies. Powerful allies who will be a surprise to everyone."

"The dragons?"

I smile. "No, even more powerful than the dragons. You'll see soon, but until then, I need you to trust that we'll win. I need you to believe in our cause. We all need to pull together but if we do, we'll be victorious."

His mind is getting stronger. He's made his decision.

"I'll be in touch soon," I say as a farewell. "Ready your forces."

I pull back and open my eyes again. The guys are still in the exact same position; no time at all seems to have passed. This kind of mind communication seems to be the same as how I talk to the other three season Gods.

"He's going to support us," I announce. "Let's deal with Hades when the time comes. Saturn... let's use him for our benefit. If we feed him some wrong information, he'll carry it right to the

Morrigan, and she's likely to believe a God more than her other spies.

"Good plan." Storm's aura is glowing with pride. "You're dealing with all of this really well."

My mother's death, he means? No, I'm not dealing with it at all. It's pushed away into a tiny, dark corner of my mind and that's where it will stay for now. I need my emotions to stay clear of it until I've succeeded in my current mission.

Killing the Morrigan.

Destroying her once and for all.

I push back the duvet and sit up, frowning at my lack of clothes.

"Your skin was healing," Crispin explains. "We didn't want it to be in contact with fabric that it might get stuck to."

I chuckle. "Nice excuse for having me naked."

"I wish we had time to enjoy the view," Frost sighs. "But you don't look like you're about to lie back down and let us make you feel good."

He's right. I wish I could, but I know I can't. There's so much to do.

"Soon," I tell him and send some loving thoughts along the bond connecting us. "Everything will be over soon and then we'll lock ourselves into my bedroom and ignore the world for a few days."

"Weeks, please," Arc demands. "Or months. We need ya."

"I need you too," I reply sadly. "Being Queen is so annoying."

Chapter Sixteen

As it turns out, a beautiful set of armour has been made for me. It's strange to wear it, but it's also kind of cool to feel this badass. It's made of snug metal plates that make my hips look curvier than they are, but there's a soft fabric inside that somehow lightens them. It doesn't feel like I'm wearing dozens of pounds worth of metal on my body, instead, it's more like the weight of a woollen coat. Two curved bits of metal hug my breasts. Whoever designed the pointy bits at the end was having a laugh. My boobs don't even look this perfectly shaped when I'm wearing a bra.

"The metal is infused with magic repellents," Frost explains as he helps me put on the shoulder guards. "You'll still need to keep up a barrier, but if something gets through, you'll be protected from minor magic attacks. It's also impenetrable to any form of weapon."

"Wait, completely impenetrable? There must be weak spots? What happens if there's a really sharp weapon?"

"Magic," is all he says as an explanation. "This will keep you as safe as it gets. The armour is made from the metal that was once part of Beira's armour, but she was taller than you, so the smiths melted it down and crafted a completely new one for you."

"Before or after the coronation?"

I don't want them to have done it after she died. That feels wrong. Her belongings should stay as they are and not be changed to fit me.

"Before. I think she knew that she would never be able to fight in a battle again, so she had it changed to protect you. She was always thinking of how to keep you safe, even though she knew you had to fight."

He wiggles the shoulder guards back and forth to make sure they're well secured.

"I think you're ready."

I shake my head. "I don't think I am."

He pulls me closer. I can't feel his touch through the thick armour, but his closeness is comforting nonetheless.

"When you woke up, you were different, Wyn. Not bad different, not good different, just changed. More aware. Sharper, somehow. I don't know how to describe it, but I can tell you how I felt. Like you were the one person I'd follow anywhere. I trust you completely because I know your heart. I know how much you care for us, for everyone in this Realm. You will lead us through the darkness and back into the light. I have absolutely no doubt about that. I'm not saying it will be easy or that there won't be losses, but I believe in you, Wyn."

I swallow hard. Don't cry, Wyn. Don't cry, not after all the beautiful things he said.

"I love you," he adds and the floodgates open. I rest my head on his shoulder as I cry and cry, my tears soaking his shirt.

I know this is the last time I'm getting this emotional. The last chance to get rid of all the pent up sadness in me. It's not the deep sadness, that one will have to stay stashed away for a while, just the sadness of what's about to happen. People will die. This isn't a game, this is war. I don't think I'd ever be completely ready for that, but Frost's words have hardened my resolve. There's nobody else who can do this. I'm the Winter Goddess, the Queen of this Realm, and I'm going to lead my people to victory.

While I was unconscious, some of the visiting dragon shifters taught our strongest mages how to create a temporary Gate. I'm glad since this means I don't have to teleport everyone and can conserve my strength.

All eleven of them are standing before me in a courtyard that I've surrounded with the yellow magic that makes it impossible for anyone to listen in. My Guardians are behind me, giving me strength.

Until now, I've stayed in the shadows, not wanting anyone to know that I'm awake. Only the Council and my Guardians knew before this moment, but it's time to show myself to the people who will be fighting and dying for the Realm.

"Are you all confident you'll be able to create a Gate and keep it open for long enough to let one battalion through?"

They all salute as an answer. I didn't know much about how the military works before, but my mother's knowledge is filling the blanks. Thanks to her, I now have all the statistics of how many soldiers we have, how many Guardians specialise in specific kinds of magic, how many weapons we have at our disposal. There are poison flasks that can be thrown, magical grenades and bombs that can make everyone freeze. At first, it looks like we're unbeatable with all these resources, but I'm aware that the Morrigan will likely have the same. Plus, she has the higher numbers. Her demons might not all be as well trained and as powerful, but they make it up with how many they are. Nobody knows for sure, but demons are known for spawning at high rates during times of war. I don't want to think about how exactly they do that. Let's hope it's cloning or something like that, not sex and baby demons.

"Good. Storm will assign each of you an officer to report to. No matter what happens, you stay with that officer and follow their commands. Once everyone is in place, your officer will be told your destination. You'll then open a Gate and make sure everyone gets there safely, before closing it again. I don't want any enemies using our Gates to enter the Palace. Understood?"

"Yes, Your Majesty!" they shout as one. Their auras are full of hope and confidence. They really believe that we're going to win this. Well, we are. I have the same confidence in my heart.

"There may be strategies that you're not aware of. If your officer asks you to bring everyone to a new location, you do that without question. Everything relies on you eleven and while you should feel that responsibility, I want you to be proud of your role."

Their auras brighten even more.

"Be ready, the signal to leave could come at any time. Don't get distracted and defend this Realm!"

I shout the last few words and a chorus of cheers responds.

"Good work," Storm whispers from behind me, before walking towards the mages and handing each of them a note with the name of their commanding officers. They don't know it yet that we're not just defending the Realm. We're also attacking another one.

Being the ones to throw the first stone leaves a bitter taste in my mouth, but it's what will give us the best chances of success. I know the Morrigan and I'm sure she won't expect us making this move. She doesn't see us as equals. She's a clever Goddess, but her superiority will be her downfall.

I go through my checklist in my head. The Council has been briefed. I've said goodbye to my father. The mages know what to do. Our forces are ready to be transported to their designated attack points. Now all I need to do is tell our allies. The Council have reassured me that all our allied Gods have their forces ready, so all they need is the time and place of where I want them to join my own army. This isn't my plan, it's what Storm and Gwain have been working on, but it needs to look like it's all me. People trust in me, their Goddess, the woman who survived an explosion that killed the old Winter Queen.

I turn to my remaining Guardians while Storm is still talking to the mages.

"Do you think we're ready?"

"Aye. Time to kick that bitch off her throne." Arc's voice is full of passion and anger. Good, that will help him in the battle.

"Yes, all the healers are standing by. Theodore will supervise them."

There was no persuading Crispin to stay with the healers and off the battlefield. He won't leave my side, and to be honest, I'm grateful to have all four men with me. I might have all these shiny new powers, but that doesn't mean I'm not afraid. Terrified, actually.

"We can do this," Frost says confidently. "I told you already and I will tell you as often as you need to hear it."

Storm joins us. "Are we doing a pep talk?"

I grimace. "No, a make-Wyn-feel-like-she's-ready-talk."

"Same thing." He grows serious. "Everyone's in position. All you need to do is contact the other Gods."

I nod. "Not here though. Hold my hand."

They do as I ask, already used to the procedure, and I teleport us onto the top of the highest tower. I like it up there. I feel like I'm away from the Palace and yet still part of it. It's freeing.

I sit down in the centre of the circular platform and focus on my magic. I know my Guardians will keep watch while I do the whole mind thing. I know that I can do it and I have my mother's memories, but it still takes me several tries until I connect with Dewi's mind.

Even though she knows I'm going to be doing this, she still shrieks in surprise. I hope it was just a mental shriek and not a physical one. I don't want her to be embarrassed.

"Everyone's ready," I tell her without further ado. "I'm going to try and send you an image of the map and your position, let me know if you get it."

I call up the map from my mind, the one Storm has shown me, complete with little flags to symbolise the places our allies are supposed to use to enter the Demon Realm. My mother is... was one of the few people who ever visited that Realm, so I had to make a few changes to the map Gwain had procured. It was like one of those old maps of Britain where the coastline is all wrong, but you can still make out the basic shape. That's what the Demon Realm map looked like. It's correct now though, thanks to my mother's memories. If I had the time, I'd get a little panicked about how her knowledge is seeping into mine, changing it, but no, I need to focus. No time to get hysterical because I feel my own self merging with a dead Goddess's consciousness.

Definitely no panicking.

I push the map towards Dewi, trying not to be too fast. I have no idea if this is going to work and melting her mind is not on my agenda. She's strong, but I'm a lot more powerful. That's not boasting, that's just a fact.

"Got it," she says much quicker than I'd expected. "Which colour am I?"

"Brown. I'm going to do the rounds and let all others know, but try and be there in two hours. I'm going to leave a tiny connection open so when you feel that activating, it's time to attack."

I can feel her assent and return to my body.

My Guardians are looking at me curiously. I smile at them.

"One down, another twenty or so to go. Could someone get me some tea?"

By the time I've contacted every single God, I'm exhausted. Not physically, not my magic, but mentally. It's like I've been at a long, drawn-out party where I had to talk to every single guest. I've done far too much socialising today. Luckily, the next people I meet are probably going to be demons that I can kill. Hurray.

I teleport us back into the Council chambers, where everyone is waiting. Gwain and Ada are dressed for battle, his armour dented in several places. I'm sure it could easily be repaired, but he might see it as a source of pride, a memory of all the wars he's won and survived.

Theodore is wearing a strange robe with dozens of pockets over his black clothes, as well as a belt full of tiny flasks.

Anthony, our new treasurer, looks a little pale, but he's wearing armour as well, just like Algonquin and Zephyr. Those two seem far too old to fight, but I remind myself that they are Guardians, immortal and likely a lot stronger than they look.

The only one who's not going to join me in the Demon Realm is Tamara who's going to oversee things from here, together with several Guardians who can communicate with their minds. They're our back up plan, in case I'm prevented from coordinating our allies myself.

"Is everyone ready?" I ask, not even bothering to sit down.

"We are, my Queen," Gwain replies formally. "The troops are ready to take their positions. All we need is your signal."

I take a deep breath. This is the moment everything will be decided. I might be sending everyone to their deaths. If this doesn't work out, the Morrigan is going to take the Winter Realm and many others and turn them into her own private hell. The balance will fail, magic will cease to exist, life will suffer.

No, this cannot happen. We need to be victorious, we will be.

"Spread the word," I tell the Council. "Let's show the Morrigan that we're not as weak as she thinks we are. Let's make her pay for what she's done."

Chapter Seventeen

Seeing everyone run through the Gates, armour glinting, weapons blazing, is exhilarating. I wait for a moment to make sure that everything is going as planned, then I turn to my four Guardians.

"Frost, tell me one last time," I ask, a sudden wave of fear spreading through me.

"I believe in you," he says simply, as if that's not one of the most precious things he's ever said to me. "You will be magnificent."

His aura pulses with pride and love as he steps forward and takes me into his arms. Once again, the armour is in the way, but his lips find mine nonetheless. I kiss him passionately, trying to keep the terrible thought at bay that's seeping into my mind. What if this is the last time I ever kiss him? What if I'll never see any of them?

I breathe in his scent, committing it to memory. My Frost.

Even after we break the kiss, I stay in his arms.

"Tonight, we'll take this further," he promises and I can hear the smile in his voice.

"My turn," Arc interrupts and pulls me away from Frost and into a rough hug. He's wearing a kilt above his metal armour as if he cannot let go of the Scottishness he was created with.

He lowers his head and kisses me hard, his lips much more demanding than Frost's. I lean into the kiss, tasting my Guardian, hoping desperately that this isn't an end, just one of many more kisses, millions of kisses in our immortal life together.

This time it's Storm who pulls me into his arms. He doesn't kiss me, he just looks at me, except that I can't see his face. It's strange, knowing he's able to look into my eyes but I am not. It's like I'm blind and yet not quite.

I don't know what he sees in my eyes, but after a minute or so, his aura changes colour, turning a fiery, passionate red.

"Be safe," he mutters and gives me the gentlest kiss ever, just a quick touch of his lips on mine, then he's gone and Crispin takes his place. Sweet, broken Crispin. I'm doing this for him, for my mum, my mother, the dragons and for everyone who's suffered at the hands of the Morrigan.

"She's going to be sorry she ever hurt you," I whisper and kiss him, showing him how much I mean it. He responds in kind, his tongue nudging mine, our bond sizzling into life, warming my heart. I can feel the connection to my guys, stronger than ever. They're here for me and I will protect them at all costs. They're mine and the Morrigan isn't getting them. She's not getting anyone. She'll be dead.

I stretch out my arms while Crispin is still holding me, and the other three men take them.

"Ready?" I ask quietly and feel their assent filtering through our bond. "Then let's kill a Goddess."

While most of our allies are starting the battle on the borders of the Demon Realm, working their way inwards, herding the demons like cattle, the guys and I teleport right into the centre. The Realm is made up of thirteen Zones, all named after jewels. Twelve of them surround the Onyx Zone like spikes on a wheel. If I know the Morrigan at all, this is where she will be, like the spider in the centre of the web.

I wasn't quite sure where best to teleport us to, so I've chosen a spot just outside the castle walls, a place I've seen in my mother's memories. In reality, the castle is much scarier though. Its ragged towers are formed like spears, reaching high into the blood red sky as if they want to pierce and destroy it. The walls are made from polished black stone; onyx, I assume. There are no windows at all, not even arrow slits. It's a strange, threatening structure that sends a clear message: get out. Well, we won't, we have a job to do.

"I'll check for demons," I tell my Guardians and extend my magic, pushing it into the air around us until it scatters and moves into all directions.

"At least ten by the main gate and hundreds within the castle. Four, no, five Gods inside. Not the Morrigan, though."

Disappointment makes my heart beat faster. She was supposed to be here. Luckily, our plan has prepared for that eventuality.

"I think it's time to give the signal."

I look at my Guardians, at their auras. All of them are exuding confidence. Seems like we've reached the point of no return.

"Keep watch while I do this."

Crispin chuckles. "I love it when she goes all dominant."

"Hey!" I playfully shove him and he laughs even more when our armour vibrates at the impact.

"Quiet," Storm warns. "We're in enemy territory now, don't be too cocky."

Annoyingly, that makes me think of the guys' body parts that I've been craving, but no, this isn't the time for my hormones to get all excited. First, we kill some demons, then we can relax and have some much-needed fun.

I close my eyes and focus on the thin, weak connections I still have with all the Gods that will be fighting on our side. If we're lucky, they're all in position already, or will be there shortly.

I pull on the connections like I usually do with my Guardians' bond, hoping desperately that this will work. There was no time to practice.

Small echoes flow back along the connections, hopefully the sign that they've received the signal and will start the assault.

I follow one of them and reach Thor. The God of Thunder immediately responds to my probing.

"There are no demons where we entered, but we're flying inland now," he reports and sends me an image of thousands of winged Guardians flying over a barren, charred landscape. The red light of the sky is reflected by their glowing wings, giving them an ethereal appearance. It's a beautiful sight. An army of angels, taking revenge on the leader of demons.

"Good. The Morrigan isn't in the Onyx castle, so if you spot her, send me a message."

I pull back and open my eyes again.

"The battle has begun," I announce, feeling very weird about saying that. It's such a grave, dramatic statement that sounds more like from a film than reality. This is really happening. Doubt creeps through my mind again, but I push it away. My Guardians believe in me, the other Gods trust me, now I just need to believe in myself.

"Do you think the Morrigan could be wherever Flora is being held?" Crispin suddenly asks.

"It would make sense," Storm agrees. "We still don't know why she took Flora, so if she needs the Spring Goddess for something, surely she'd stick close to her?"

I swallow hard. I have a bad feeling about this.

I connect with my spread out magic again to check if one of the Gods in the castle is Flora, but of course, we aren't that lucky. However, now that we're in the Demon Realm, I might be able to sense her, if she's not too far away.

Before I can try that, my magic alerts me to movement inside the castle.

"They must have been alerted to the attacks," I tell the Guardians. "Demons are moving in the castle and so are the Gods."

A moment later, we hear the large castle gate open and a cacophony of shouts and shrieks fills the air. The demons are leaving their fortress to go into battle.

"Two of the Gods have disappeared, they must be able to teleport. One of them is moving fast, out of the gate, and... he's coming here!"

Immediately, my Guardians jump into action, surrounding me protectively. It's a sweet gesture, but I don't need their protection.

The God running towards us doesn't feel familiar. He's not one we've hosted at the Palace before. Wait, not he. She.

"That's Nyx!" Frost hisses. "The Goddess of Night. I didn't know she was still alive, I hadn't heard of her for decades."

"She must have been hiding out in the shadows with the Morrigan," Crispin mutters. "I met her when I was still... her prisoner. Let's try and make this quick, she's devious and likes to play with her prey."

I feel sick at that thought. People taking pleasure in the suffering of others are the worst, whether they're humans, Guardians or Gods.

The Goddess is almost upon us and I create an invisible barrier just in front of her. When she runs against it and crashes to the ground, I have to suppress a laugh.

She'd be beautiful with her glowing dark skin and her long black hair, if the corners of her mouth weren't downturned in a sour expression and her brows weren't drawn together in a scowl. She's cursing in an unknown language, but it's clear she's not exactly saying nice things to me.

She jumps up and dark fog starts to swirl around her outstretched arms.

"Nightmare magic," Crispin explains from behind me. "Don't let it touch you."

"I have no intention of doing so."

I make the barrier visible as an icy sphere surrounding us. I've learned my lesson and made sure that the protection extends to above and below us. There's no way for her magic to enter our safe space. Now that the defence is sorted, let's start the offence. I decide on water and ice magic, my mother's elements. This is in her honour. Unbeknownst to Nyx, I conjure ten sharp icicles behind her, pointing at her back. This time, I'm not wanting to start the attack though. I want to give her a chance to surrender. Call me weak, call me naive, but I don't want to turn into a murderer.

"Where is the Morrigan?" I ask calmly, keeping my body as relaxed as possible, as if I wasn't ready to skewer her any second now.

Nyx sneers. "I can bring you to her. Dead or alive, it's your choice. Just lower your barrier and I'll show you where she is."

I laugh. "Do you think I'm stupid? Tell me now or fight."

"Not as stupid as your mother, but-"

She doesn't finish. She's dead.

I let go of the icicles that have pierced her lifeless body and she crumples to the floor.

"Did you just kill a Goddess?" Storm asks. "It shouldn't be this easy."

I'm wondering the same thing, but then the answer comes to me as if it's always been there.

"My mother created her," I say slowly, speaking as the thoughts enter my mind. "Beira couldn't kill her creations, but I can. I know their weak spots because of my mother's memories, but I'm not bound by the same laws. I think if I have the *intention* of killing a God she created, then I can do it even with normal magic. I don't need poison or special knives like Angus had to use."

"That's a tiny bit scary," Frost mutters. "Let's try not to make that public knowledge. We don't want our allies to fear you."

I look down at the dead Goddess and nod. "Yes, I don't really want to think about it myself. I have no intention of killing any other Gods unless I need to."

"Except for the Morrigan," Crispin corrects.

"Yes, except for her." I concentrate on my magic. "The castle is mostly empty. It would be the perfect time to capture it, but it's not like we're here to conquer this Realm. To be honest, I'm happy to leave it to the demons once the Morrigan is defeated."

"Yes, Queen of the Underworld doesn't suit you," Frost snickers. "Let's stick to the nicer Realms."

I'm about to reply, but darkness falls and I'm back in the black room that's become so familiar.

"Hey," I say lightly. "How are things?"

"The Morrigan just commanded me to come to her aid," Angus says, glee swinging in his voice. "I'm going to follow her call, but not like she thinks."

"Where is she?" I ask immediately.

"With me," Flora whispers weakly. She sounds like she's in pain, even though we're in this safe place.

"What is she doing?" I try to sound calm and keep the fear at bay. If Flora is harmed, everything could be lost. We need all four of us to keep the balance.

"Playing," Flora replies grimly. "She's having fun."

I don't ask any more. If Flora doesn't want to tell us the specifics, that's fine. We all deserve privacy in our pain. There's one thing that doesn't quite make sense though.

"Angus, how did she command you to come to her when she's torturing Flora right now?"

"She spoke to me a few minutes ago, I swear. The same way she always does, in my mind. She seemed very angry."

"That's because we're attacking her from all sides." I'm pushing my suspicions of Angus's statement to one side for the moment. There's nothing I can do about it now. If he wants to betray us, I can't stop him. I just have to hope that there's a logical explanation of how the Morrigan was doing both things at the same time.

I turn my attention to Flora again. "Don't worry, she won't be able to stay with you for much longer. There are more than twenty forces invading her Realm at the same time. She'll have to coordinate her defences once she realises the scale of the attack."

"Good." She sounds exhausted. "Are you coming for me?"

"We are," Dewi confirms, speaking for the first time. "I'm following the connection between us. You were right, Spring and Autumn attract each other. I can feel you, faintly, and I'm flying there as soon as possible. Don't be scared if a flock of dragon suddenly appears."

Flora laughs softly. "I'm in a dungeon, I'm afraid I won't be able to see you."

"You will, after," Dewi promises."

"Dewi, I need to go there too, but I don't have a connection like you have. If you send me an image of your location though I'll be able to teleport and follow you."

"Dragons fly faster than Guardians," Dewi says but sends me a mental image nonetheless. There are mountains beneath her, high and sharp, not covered in snow but in a red dust that seems to suck in the light from the burning skies. There's a black lake that they're flying towards. That seems a good landmark to zone in on.

"I'll meet you at the lake. If we can't fly fast enough, we can always ride on you."

I can feel Dewi's outrage, but the blackness disappears and I'm back with my Guardians.

They must have noticed that I was gone because they're all staring at me. In the past, I was only gone for a second or two when these strange meetings occurred, but I guess the Guardians know me well enough to notice any change in my behaviour.

"How do you feel about a little race against dragons?" I ask them with a grin.

All of their auras light up in anticipation at that challenge.

"Dewi is heading to Flora and we're going to follow her. I know where she is, so we can teleport there. Ready?"

"Will we appear on land or in the air?" Storm asks. I hadn't actually thought about the possibility of teleporting us into thin air.

"Is that possible?"

"Other Gods do it." Storm shrugs. "I'm sure you can do it too."

He's already spread his beautiful wings and the others follow his lead. I do the same, relishing at the feeling of freedom expanding my wings always gives me. I really need to fly more, but I've not really had the chance recently.

"Okay then... If we fall, try and catch each other." I smile and hold out my arms like always and teleport us as soon as they touch me.

Air. Falling. No ground. I'm going to crash. Wyn splatter in the Demon Realm, what a fitting end.

"Fly, Wyn! Remember yer wings!"

Arc circles me, his wings beating strongly. He looks ready to dive and catch me, but he's reminded me of how to fly. Silly me, forgetting the essentials. I flap my wings and stop falling. Phew.

"The dragons are approaching!" Storm shouts and I turn around, changing the angle of my wings so I can hover in place.

It's a tremendous sight. At least fifty dragons of all shapes and sizes are racing towards us, their wings so majestic that I need to suppress a gasp. They are formidable, an enemy I really wouldn't want to meet in battle. Good thing they're on our side.

Dewi is flying at the front of the flock, her blue scales glittering in the reddish air. She's by far the largest of them all and blue smoke is rising from her nostrils. Did she communicate with us while flying? I'm glad she didn't fall; her weight must make it hard to stay in the air without flapping constantly.

"They're fast," Frost observes with a hint of admiration in his voice. "But we're fast too."

I doubt that we can match the dragons' speed, but we won't know without trying. The Guardians are a lot faster than me though. They're physically stronger and have more practice. Oh well. Here goes.

As one, we rise to match the dragons' altitude and prepare to meet them in flight. Dewi roars a greeting, tiny ice crystals steaming from her toothy maw.

Then they're upon us, surrounding us. Even the smallest dragon is at least three times as long as I am, not counting their spiked tails. Their wings are thin membranes surrounded by strong bones and muscle, not at all like the almost translucent fairy wings of Guardians. They don't wait, they just keep on flying and I beat my wings hard to keep up. Even so, they quickly pass me by. My tiny wingspan is no match against theirs. My Guardians stay by my side, even though I know they could fly a lot faster. They're staying to not make me look weak.

"Come on, race them!" I tell them when I see the impatience swirling in their auras. "You know you want to."

"I'll stay with her," Crispin says and the others fly off after I give them an encouraging nod. Storm is the fastest, but his twin isn't far behind. Arc almost matches them, but he's heavier and his bulk is holding him back.

Storm reaches the dragon furthest at the back and overtakes him, but he doesn't manage to progress to further in the dragon formation. We're outwinged.

A dark green dragon breaks away from the flock and turns, flying towards Crispin and me. She circles around us and the hovers just beneath me. An invitation to ride on her? I didn't expect any of the dragons to offer that willingly. From the little I know about dragons, they're incredibly proud beings.

I let myself sink until I'm just above her, then spread my legs and drop the final few feet. Her back is warm and the scales are surprisingly soft. I keep my wings extended at first, but with some air magic wrapped around me, I feel safe enough to fold them away and ride on the dragon.

Wow. I'm riding on a dragon. An actual dragon with scales and wings and a very spiky tail. Life really has become crazy. A magical adventure. With a body count, hopefully in form of demons, not Guardians and Gods.

"Thank you!" I shout and the dragon nods her head in response. I have no idea how I know that she's female, but I take it as a fact. Crispin is flying by my side, just about managing to keep up. No dragon has offered to let him ride on them, so they must be confident in his ability to fly alongside them. The other three Guardians let themselves fall back a little until they're flying to the left of me.

It's exhilarating and I can't resist whooping a little. Not too loud, I don't want the dragons to think I'm crazy. I'm the Winter Goddess now, I can't afford to be childish anymore. But a little shout of joy...

"Woohooo!" I scream and the Guardians laugh. Even the dragon I'm riding on chuckles, making her entire body vibrate beneath my thighs. I wrap my air magic a little tighter, in case the dragon decides to make any sudden movements.

Once I've got used to the feeling of riding a fricking dragon, I look down to see where we are. We've left the mountains behind and are currently traversing a bleak, boring landscape full of nothing but brown and black stone and marshland. There's no sign of life, a few ruins, but not a single occupied demon settlement.

This must be an area avoided even by demons. The perfect place to hide.

It's becoming hotter though. The sky above is bright red and the clouds look like smoke that's rising from a fire somewhere. I follow their path... and yes, it is smoke. From a big, big fire. Well, a volcano. Same thing. And it's erupting. The closer we get, the more detail I can make out. Lava is running down the mountain in wide streams, culminating in a large lava lake at the bottom which surrounds the mountain like a moat. What's strange though is that the lake is still burning; none of the lava seems to be cooling and growing black.

The smell of ash is filling the air and I make sure to keep a filter made from some air magic in front of my face. I neither want that smell in my nose nor any ash particles in my eyes.

"Look!" Arc suddenly shouts. "There's a building on the mountain!"

That can't be. Who would build on an active volcano?

Well, easy. Demons.

But there it is, a black structure that's both part of the mountain and separate from it. Lava is flowing over the castle walls, but they don't seem damaged at all. The perfect fortress. Surrounded by lava, the walls unscalable. The only way in is through the air. I bet they have some good defences there as well. We're about to find out.

The dragons in front of us start to descend. This seems to be our destination. Great. We're going to land on a volcano. Could someone wake me up, please? This can't be real.

I hold tight as my own dragon begins to tilt downwards. The steep angle she's taking is making me queasy. If I didn't have my magic, I'd no doubt have already fallen to my death. Next time, maybe the dragons could supply some reins and a saddle? I guess there won't be a next time though. This is a once in a lifetime opportunity and I should be enjoying it... and I did, but now... The dragon swerves right and I almost lose my grip. My stomach lurches as the world tilts and black walls appear all around us. We're in the castle. How were there no defences? That's suspicious, very much so.

We land more elegantly than I expected from such a large creature. It's hot here, incredibly hot, and even some cooling air magic doesn't quite get rid of the heat. I slide down the dragon's side, grateful to be back on solid ground. Which suddenly trembles. How safe is this place? Could the volcano destroy it?

I smile grimly when I realise what I'm thinking. I'm about to confront the Morrigan. A little earthquake is the least of my worries.

Chapter Eighteen

My Guardians land beside me and immediately surround me in their favourite defensive formation.

"Guys, I can look after myself," I complain, but they don't budge. I sigh and head towards the front of the dragon flock. All of them are still in their dragon shape, except for one. Dewi. Her hair is wrapped around her head like a crown and her body is covered in an armour that looks like it's made from dragon scales. It's beautiful and probably very efficient. And if she's lucky, it's even lighter than my own. I've almost got used to the feeling of wearing my armour, but after being on the dragon, my bones are a little stiff.

How much time has passed since I spoke to the other Gods? Fifteen minutes perhaps? Twenty? Let's hope the Morrigan is still here. And Flora. Alive. I don't think I can hope for unharmed, not after what she said earlier, but at least alive. Crispin is here with me and he's the best healer in my Realm. He'll look after her.

"She's here, I can feel her. Down below, not far. She's weak though. We need to hurry."

"Can your people keep watch up here?" I ask and she nods. "I can feel demons all around us but for some reason, they haven't reacted yet. How did we get through their defences? There must have been some?"

Dewi grins. "Dragon scales repel magic. You must have been close enough to us not to be affected."

"That's a useful skill to have," Storm says in surprise. Seems I'm not the only one who didn't know this before. These dragons turn out to be even more useful allies by the second.

"Lead on," I tell her and Dewi's smile disappears, giving way to a more guarded, serious expression.

"I could probably teleport us there, but who knows how many demons are waiting for us inside the castle. Safer to take the longer route."

I nod in agreement and she heads towards a door in one of the walls, almost invisible because it's the same stone as everything else. I'm keeping my magic at the ready. Not seeing a single demon so far is making me very suspicious. There are no demons on the walls because there's lava there that would burn them alive, but still, there are two doors leading into the courtyard we're in and neither has opened.

I feel like we're being watched, but my magic doesn't show anyone nearby. Strange. And very, very worrying.

Dewi opens the door, her hands extended, ready to throw magic at whoever is awaiting us, but the dark corridor is empty.

"There are demons below us, but none on this level," I whisper. Dewi walks a little faster and we hurry to follow. When we reach some stairs leading down, she stops and I concentrate on my magic again.

"Ten demons waiting for us at the bottom of the stairs. More up ahead, but I don't think there are any really powerful ones."

"We'll deal with them," Storm announces and steps forward, followed by the other Guardians.

I'm about to protest, but Dewi holds me back.

"Let them. They need to feel needed," she whispers. "It's the same with Agierth. Sometimes, you just need to step back and let them do their protector thing."

I sigh and stay where I am, although I still keep my magic at the ready. Just because I'm not with my Guardians doesn't mean I'm leaving them to fight on their own. I'm not that kind of woman.

Screams come from the other end of the stairs, but those aren't the voices of my Guardians. They are demon screams, raw and full of pain. Good riddance. I wish I could feel empathy for them, but after one of them abducted my parents and tortured them in the process, I no longer can. Right now, they're nothing but obstacles in my way to reach the Morrigan.

"Clear!" Storm shouts from below and I hurry down the stairs, followed by Dewi. I ignore the corpses on the ground and the blood stains on my men's armour. They are not important.

"Two more floors down," Dewi informs us. "Flora's in pain. Our connection is getting stronger, I can almost feel the pain myself now." She shudders visibly. "Let's hurry up."

She doesn't let the Guardians take the lead this time. Instead, she rushes ahead and only stops when I tell her that more demons are coming. There are five of them and I kill them with an icicle each through the heart. Nobody says a word and we hurry on. This is war, there's no time for sentimentality.

Twenty dead demons and two more staircases later, we arrive in the dungeons. They're just like you'd imagine prison cells in an evil fortress to look like. Rusty bars in front of dark, small compartments. It reeks of pain and decay. I suppress a shiver.

"Is she close?" I ask Dewi and the Goddess nods.

"Just up ahead."

A moment later, a scream confirms her words. Flora.

We run towards the pained wails that echo through the stone corridor. Suddenly, a demon steps in our way. He's fat, there's no other word for it. His belly is bulging over a leather belt from which hang... are those shrunken... ehm... cocks? I avert my eyes and focus on the rest of him instead. He's bald, but there's a shimmering green rash all over his grey skin. Weeping sores cover his face and one of his eyes is missing. This might be the ugliest demon I've ever seen.

"The Mistress promised me some playtime," he growls in a raspy, disgustingly sultry voice. "So good of you to come."

"Who are you?" Dewi asks, her magic flaring around her arms, ready to be unleashed.

"My name is Cristian and I'm the Morrigan's personal representative in this Realm."

I snicker loudly. "Not for much longer."

He turns his eyes on me... ehm, his eye. It's bloodshot and surrounded by tiny warts. Yucky. It's almost a pity that demons don't have an aura to hide their faces. For once, I'd quite like to not see someone's expression.

"Who wants to be first?" he asks and suddenly, a large spiked mace appears in his hand. There's dried blood on the spikes, presumably a souvenir from his last victim.

"How about you?" I ask and shove some icicles towards him. They never reach him though, breaking into a million tiny shards a foot in front of him. There's a barrier I didn't notice. How did I not realise? I concentrate but I still can't feel anything in the air between us. Strange, does that mean I can't recognise demon magic? That's a scary thought.

At least I can sense them... well, not this one. He seems to be more powerful than the demons we've encountered in this castle before. I hope he's the only one of his kind.

I conjure some more icicles and fire them at him from behind, but again, there's an invisible barrier that stops them. He laughs at my efforts. This is becoming tedious. If ice won't work, then I'll show him that I have other magic at my disposal.

I create a giant fireball and throw it at him from above, while at the same time funnelling a small tornado all around him to dispel the barrier. His grin disappears and makes way to a concentrated frown. His barrier is finally giving way and the first sparks of my fireball reach him. He screams as flames lick at his skin. Some of the sores on his face burst as they get in contact with the fire and his wails increase. He's looking even more disgusting now, with burns and weird slime covering his skin. Let's end this quickly so I don't have to look at him anymore.

I fan the flames with my magic and throw an icicle at his heart for good measure. This time, it reaches its target and with a squelching sound, embeds itself in the demon's chest. He stares at me in surprise, then crumples to the floor, dead.

"What a weirdo," Dewi mutters and steps over the corpse, her aura full of disgust. A cry from the end of the corridor makes us run again. Flora sounds like she's in agony. The stupid demon distracted us for too long.

We reach a thick wooden door. It's locked, but Storm blasts it open with his wind magic until it splinters and bangs open. I'm the first to step into the room and have to stop the bile from rising in my throat. We're inside a torture chamber.

Strange instruments litter the walls and shelves, iron chains hang from the ceiling and very painful looking contraptions are standing all around. I recognise an Iron Maiden in the corner, even though I know that they were never actually used on Earth, they were a Victorian invention for curiosity cabinets. I push that useless fact from my mind. This really isn't the time.

A large metal table is in the centre of the room and on it, Flora, her arms and legs shackles so she's in a spread eagle position. She's naked, too, and I can't even imagine the humiliation she must be experiencing. She's a Goddess, and here she is, completely exposed and at someone else's mercy.

Her face is covered in bruises and sweat, and there are bloody lash marks all over her body. She's suffered. All I want is to free her and take her into my arms, healing her wounds, but there's one tiny problem to deal with first. The person who did this to her. No, not a person. A monster.

"Oh look, we have guests."

The Morrigan materialises in front of the torture table, dressed in a long black gown and wearing a silver crown. Look at that, she fancies herself a Queen already. Not if I can help it.

"This ends now," I growl and create a barrier all around us. I know Dewi could probably create her own, but I'm the most powerful one of all of us.

"Oh yes, it certainly will." She laughs. "I've waited for you to come and try and free your friend. Isn't she pretty? I've had a lot of fun with her."

Rage overwhelms all rational thought and I throw all the magic I have at her. Fire, wind, ice, water, even a mental attack. Most of it crashes against a barrier she's created, but one of my weapons reaches her.

She gasps in pain and looks down at herself. Her gaze wanders to me, her eyes widened in shock, then she keels over, the icicle embedded in her heart. Red blood is flowing from the wound, drenching her dress. I want to cheer and celebrate, but something is wrong. This was too easy. Far too easy. If it was this simple to kill the Morrigan, someone would have already done it.

"Stay on your guard," I whisper to the others and use my magic to feel around the room. "This isn't over yet."

Crispin bends down beside the Morrigan's body and runs his hands over it, his healing magic springing into action.

"She's dead," he confirms, but then his aura turns the turquoise colour of surprise. "She's... No, this can't be. She's a Guardian. The Morrigan isn't a Goddess."

Suddenly, everything makes sense. Why she was so easy to kill. How she was able to speak to Angus and be in Flora's dungeon at the same time.

"That's because this isn't the real Morrigan," I say slowly. "This was a clone, like the Crispin imposters."

A flash of light fills the room, followed by an amused cackle in a very familiar voice.

The Morrigan appears from a cloud of smoke, clapping loudly. "Finally. Well done, sweetie. I'm glad you got rid of her so quickly, killing dragons was getting boring."

Dewi screams in anger and rage, and suddenly, there's a dragon by my side, only a fraction of her usual size, but large enough to be a formidable foe. I didn't know dragons could control their size, but it sure comes in handy in a confined space such as this room. She bares her teeth and a stream of icy breath hurtles towards the Morrigan, but she easily deflects it, laughing as if this was all a game.

"I'm going to enjoy having three Goddesses stuffed in my museum," she cackles. "You, Wyn, will be the centrepiece. I'll make dear little Crispin clean your dead body daily so you won't gather dust."

"What an honour." I sneer. "But I'm afraid you're not going to be here for long enough to do that."

I pull at the bond that connects me to my Guardians, the signal we agreed. When we planned how to take down the Morrigan, we didn't think Dewi would be in the room, so she's not aware of our plan. I hope she'll catch on though.

Storm and Frost let out battle cries and run at the Morrigan, their swords blazing. She swats them away like flies, but it's enough of a distraction for Arc to launch a mental attack.

Beira created the Morrigan to have incredible physical and magical powers, but she didn't give her particularly impressive mental strength. She frowns, but then decides that Arc doesn't pose a threat to her. A sword appears in her hand and she swings it around a few times, almost playfully. Storm stalks her from behind, but without turning around, she sends a ball of black magic that crashes into his chest, throwing him against the wall. He looks dazed, but he gets up and joins his brother. We all know that they have no chance against her, but they're just there to keep her occupied for now.

I'm busy weaving a net of magic, made of all the elements I have control over, even earth, the most volatile of them all. While I'm doing that, Arc is still trying to weaken her mental barriers, while Crispin has run to Flora's side, his hands already forming patterns over her injured body. He gives me a nod. Good, she'll be alright.

Dewi roars again and launches herself at the Morrigan – and slams against an invisible barrier that wasn't there moments ago. She wails in pain, blood running down her face. She growls in anger and pushes against the barrier, her claws raking against it. It's too strong, but the dragon doesn't give in.

My net is almost done when the Morrigan suddenly laughs. It's the worst possible sound. She extends a hand, her fingers stretched into claws, and points at Crispin. He freezes, terror filling his aura. I don't know if she's using magic on him or if it's just a mind fuck, but Crispin has stopped healing Flora and is now slowly moving toward the Morrigan.

"That's it, my pet," she purrs. "Come to mummy. I've missed you."

I want to throw up in disgust. Frost and Storm are trying to distract her, but with a flick of her other hand, both are flung against the wall and stay there, suspended against the stone, unable to move. Dewi is still trying to get through the barrier and Arc's got his eyes closed, focussing on breaking the Morrigan's mind. I'm the only one left.

I complete the final knot of my magic net and throw it at the Morrigan. Miraculously, it passes through the barrier, just like I'd hoped. It's too many different kinds of magic at once, and it confuses the barrier. As soon as the net touches the Morrigan, she screams in pain. Her hold on Storm and Frost breaks and they fall to the floor, weak but conscious.

Crispin has stopped moving towards his creator, but he's not retreating either.

The Morrigan tries to get the net off her, but whenever she uses one kind of magic against it, it changes. This was Algonquin's idea, something he'd read about in the library.

I focus on the net to figure out what magic is most harmful to the Morrigan. Earth and fire. I smile. Earth is difficult in here without toppling the castle, but fire is easy. We're surrounded by an active volcano, and fire magic is permeating the air around me.

I slowly change the configuration of the net and add some more fire magic. Flames begin to flicker all around the Morrigan and she curses as they touch her skin.

"You have fire magic." Her eyes are wide as she stares at the flames licking on her dress. "Your mother didn't."

I push more magic into the fire. "I'm not my mother."

I can see the moment the penny drops. She knew my mother couldn't kill her. She relied on that still to be true. She thought we were here just to capture her. I almost want to laugh at her disbelief.

"You won't succeed," she hisses and suddenly, black magic surrounds her, quenching the flames. Oh no, you don't. I grasp more magic from deep inside of me and pour it into the remains of the net. The Morrigan's succeeding in not letting it burn her, but she doesn't have the strength to go on the offensive again. Just how I want to have her.

"Crispin?" I shout. "Do you want to do it?"

At first, he doesn't respond and I'm about to ask one of the other guys when he nods slowly. Like in a trance, he moves towards the Morrigan, catching the sword that Storm throws him. She turns to him, shock reflecting on her face. She knows this is the end.

My magic is fighting me, almost spent, but I force her to keep the flames alive, trapping the Morrigan in place. It's not been a long fight, but I've never used this much magic at once. My body is getting weaker and I feel myself sway, but then Dewi is there, steadying me.

Crispin stops in front of the Morrigan, the tip of his sword pointing at her chest.

"I've been wanting to do this for a long time," he whispers. "I really hope there's no afterlife."

My vision begins to flicker, but I can't stop now. More magic is needed.

"Now!" I shout just when my grip on my magic loosens. Crispin lunges forward, the sword slicing into the Morrigan's chest, ripping through flesh and piercing her black heart.

I smile and crumble to the ground, unable to stand any longer. The flicker in front of my eyes changes and suddenly, a flash of light erases the auras that have hidden my Guardian's faces from me. I can see them again.

For about two seconds, before I'm thrown into the dark room without warning.

"Is she dead?" Angus asks before anyone else can say something. "The demons suddenly stopped fighting. We weren't sure if it's a trick or not."

"Yes, she's dead," I say, smiling. I rub my eyes, unable to believe that we didn't just defeat the Morrigan, but that I also got my old vision back. I'll be able to see them properly again. Look into their eyes. Admire their faces.

I feel free for the first time in ages. Despite all the work that still needs doing, a massive weight has been lifted from my shoulders. The Morrigan is dead. My mothers have been avenged.

Now, we can finally live in peace.

Epilogue

One week later

I wish I could say that we all just went home and had a cup of tea. No, there was still work to do. Some of the demons didn't lay down their weapons, and neither did some of the Morrigan's allies. While we'd been busy fighting her clone, she'd called her allied Gods and they came with their armies. The battle raged for two days until the last God was defeated. There were losses on both sides, but not as heavy as they could have been had the Morrigan still been there to control her demons.

Algonquin died in battle, killed by a higher demon who'd crept up on him from behind. Ever since we got back, Zephyr has been locked inside his chambers, refusing to open the door even for me. I've decided to let him grieve in peace while making sure he knows I'm there to support him. Luckily, he's been the only one of my close allies who died. Some are wounded, including Gwain who is nursing an injury to his back that almost killed him, but Crispin says they'll all recover.

All in all, we really have achieved a victory. Most of the husbands and wives of those who fought in the battle were able to welcome home their loved ones.

Dewi is mourning several of her dragons, and I've promised to attend the official mourning ceremony in her Realm soon. First though, there's a funeral here that I need to go to.

Beira is being cremated today and I'm so not ready. There was no body when my mum died, so I see it as the funeral for both of my mothers, by birth and adoption. How blessed was I to have two mums, even if I didn't always see it like that. I wish I'd had more time to spend with Beira. The memories in my mind sometimes make it feel like she's talking to me from beyond the veil, but I know that isn't really her. Still, the knowledge that I'm carrying a part of her within me helps with the grief.

"She'd be so proud of you."

Tamara enters the room, wearing a black dress similar to my own. A silver snowflake brooch rests above her bosom, a sign of her love for Beira. The crown weighs heavily on my head, another reminder that I'm on my own now. No mother to hold my hand and guide me. I have my Council and my advisors, but it's not the same. Tamara is the only one of them who understands me completely. Ada, too, but she's left for the Dragon Realm, saying she's got some unfinished business there. Two of her men were injured in the battle, but Crispin managed to heal them pretty quickly. They won't even be left with scars.

Not physical ones, anyway. I think most of us carry an assortment of mental scars. Seeing the blood, the dying, the cruelty of the demons; it all leaves a trace. I've been having nightmares, but having the Guardians with me makes them better. I've kept them close, not letting them stray too far from me. The fear of losing them now that the battle is over is irrational, I know that, but I can't help it. They are fine with my clinginess though, especially at night.

I smile when I think of yesterday evening, how we all ended up on the floor, our limbs entwined, our souls connected by kisses and gentle touches. I did say I'd lock myself into my chambers with them to have some alone time, but there's too much to do. There are going to be trials against those who allied with the Morrigan. Negotiations with Angus will start soon to draw up new contracts that will ensure no more war between our Realms. There might even be trade agreements. I don't think I'll ever be friends with Angus, but for the moment, he seems content to stick to his own Realm and keep the balance. Dewi has helped a lot with that. She's not just his step-daughter, but also a Goddess who's part of our quartet of seasons. She gives him two reasons to not start a war again any time soon.

"We should go," Tamara reminds me gently and I turn to her, nodding. I need to be strong now. Half the Realm has assembled to bid their Mother farewell, and I'll be the one to light the pyre. It's an old-fashioned ceremony, not at all like a funeral on Earth, but the memories and knowledge Beira endowed me with will hopefully guide me through it.

"I'm ready."

I'm not, but let's pretend I am.

I take her hand and teleport us onto Bald Peak, a low but wide hill not far from the Palace. Thousands of people are assembled here, forming concentric circles around the large wooden funeral pyre. On it, Beira's remains are wrapped in a golden cloth, embroidered with tiny silver snowflakes. Most people are wearing snowflake brooches to honour not just Beira, but all the dead of the Winter Realm. She may be the one on the pyre, but we're remembering all the battle's victims today.

I take my place in front of the pyre, where my father and my Guardians are already waiting for me. They're wearing black suits, even Arc. This may be the first time I've seen him without a kilt.

"You okay?" Crispin asks and I nod, my eyes fixed on the pyre. I don't want to look at the crowd and meet anyone's eyes. The other Gods form the closest circle, most of them familiar, some strangers who stayed neutral during the battle. They've all come to say farewell to my mother. Blaze is standing next to Ada and her men, his horn covered in black gauze as a sign of respect. He didn't take part in the battle, but he helped carry messages back and forth with his unique teleporting magic. I hope he's here to stay, not because of his sparklies, but because I like him as a non-person.

I take a deep breath and use some magic to enhance my voice so all can hear me.

"Today we honour Beira, the Mother of Gods, the Queen of the Winter Realm, the Goddess who kept watch over all life from the dawn of time. She may have left her mortal body behind, but she will always keep guard over this Realm through those who've been touched by her grace."

I step forward until I almost touch the pyre. I conjure a fire spiral and let it fly high into the sky. It shines down on us together with the pale winter sun.

"I, Wynter, the daughter of Beira and the new Winter Queen, will light the pyre and release my mother so magic may take her home."

I lower the fire spiral and make it wider so it surrounds the pyre. This is the moment. Be strong, Wyn. You can do this.

I close my eyes for a moment and let the fire touch the pyre. I can't bear to look. I lift my head and open my eyes again, watching as the first smoke begins to drift up and form a beautiful pattern on the clear sky.

I raise my voice again and recite the ancient blessing.

May the road rise to meet you;
May the wind be always at your back;
May the sun shine warm upon your face;
May the snow fall softly upon your lands.
Until we meet again,
May you find rest and peace in your eternal slumber.

Tears run down my face by the time I finish. The pyre is burning brightly now and I can barely make up my mother's body. This really is the end.

Around me, people start to sing the same blessing I just recited, their voices lifting to the heavens. My heart aches at the sound and the beauty of the emotion expressed by it.

My mother may be gone, but her spirit lives on in everyone who's standing on this hill with me. I step back and immediately, my Guardians surround me, hugging me from all sides. They hold me in their arms until the fire has died out and nothing remains but ashes.

I teleport us back into my chambers. Tamara leaves us after giving me both a hug and a knowing smile. I sit down on my bed and take off my crown, using some magic to deposit it on the sideboard. Another swirl of magic removes my black dress, leaving me in just my underwear.

"You did well," Storm says, his eyes gentle and full of emotion. I'm still getting used to being able to see their faces again. I forgot how beautiful they all are, each in their own way. "She'd be proud of you."

I smile. "I know. It doesn't make it any easier though."

"How can we make it better?" Crispin asks and sits down by my side. He wraps an arm around my waist and pulls me close. My naked skin rubs against his clothes in an annoying way. I make them all naked. Now we're equal.

"Give us some warning next time?" Arc grumbles but then he laughs. "I much prefer it like that. Trousers chafe."

"It was your decision not to wear your kilt," Frost chuckles. "I know how much you like to feel the wind down there."

Arc grins. "I like to feel other things there too."

I beckon him to come closer, but he looks a little unsure.

"Are ye sure?"

"I think sex at funerals is an Earth tradition, but I'm the Queen and I can do what I like. And right now, I want to be with my Guardians. Now, let me feel you."

He nods and steps forward until his knees touch mine. I take his cock into my hands as if it's the most precious thing. Well, it is. All of them are precious. Not because of their manly bits, but because of their souls, their hearts.

I rub him gently while Crispin takes off my bra.

"I love your boobs," he mutters and lowers his mouth to them, sucking on one nipple. Frost climbs onto the bed behind me and runs his lips along the nape of my neck, pressing rows upon rows of kisses on my skin. I shiver at his touch.

Storm is still standing a few feet away from us, watching with a smile. I lock eyes with him as Frost slips a hand under my panties and begins to draw his fingers over my bud in small circles, making me gasp softly with each touch. These men will be the death of me.

I'm still looking at Storm, not able to take my eyes away from his passionate gaze that's full of fire and promises. The other three are worshipping my body while I'm still rubbing Arc's cock, eliciting groans from him that make me only want to increase my pace. I want to make them all feel good, just like they're making me feel amazing.

We're made for each other, four Guardians and their Goddess. Once, I thought I didn't deserve them, but now I know that we deserve each other. We all have our strengths and weaknesses, and we fit together like a perfect puzzle, increasing strengths and making up for weaknesses. We're one.

The bond flares up at that thought and sparks dance before my eyes. No, they're not just in my mind, they're real. Silver sparkles are filling the room and we all stop and stare. They swirl around like a gentle snow storm, then slowly begin to form a circle around us. As if by magic, Storm is pushed towards the rest of us and the sparkles swirl faster, encompassing us.

Something nudges my mind, a memory of my mother's. Wow.

"Guys?" I ask and they all turn to me, their faces illuminated by the light of the silver particles. "You'll have to say two words for this to work."

They all look at me cluelessly.

I smile. "The bond has decided that we're ready. It's... ehm... a marriage ceremony. Except that we have magic conduct it."

Their expressions mirror my own surprise and shock.

"So... it wants us to say the words. The two words that will make it real."

Crispin's eyes widen, then he smiles. "I do."

A group of sparkles branch of from the main circle and surround his head like a halo.

"I do," Storm and Frost say at the same time, like the brothers they are. The magic marks them as ready just like it did to Crispin.

Arc is the last one. He looks me in the eyes and takes my hands in his.

"I do."

The sparkles around us turn a bright gold and become so fast that they're blurring into lines.

Only one thing left to do.

I take a deep breath and let my magic caress all four of them. These words are so simple, yet they're the most important words I'll ever say. And I'll never, ever regret them.

"I do."

And that's how I make them mine. My men, my Royal consorts.

My Guardians.

~ The End ~

This is the end of Wynter's story... or is it?
Revisit the Winter Palace in Samhain Goddess, a novella set
several months after the events of this book. Ghosts, Gods and
frilly dresses - Wyn has a new mystery to solve.

If you enjoyed this book, please consider leaving a review!
Subscribe to my newsletter for all the lastest releases, offers and
looks behind the scenes:
skyemackinnon.com/newsletter.

Author's Note

In July 2017, I published my very first book, Call of Winter, the first part of the Winter Princess serial. I was a new author, nobody had ever heard of me, and I was only just starting to be active on social media. Not the best starting conditions, but for some reason, people bought the book. Lots of you amazing readers took a chance and started reading Wyn's story.

Overnight, I was suddenly a bestselling author with readers from all over the world who wrote reviews, sent me messages, demanded more. Some even volunteered to help out with my Facebook group and others started beta reading for me. It was all a bit overwhelming, and yet terribly exciting at the same time. I was working for a university back then and spent all my evenings and weekends writing - goodbye social life. I'd been wondering whether it was going to be worth it, but having even just one happy reader totally made it worthwhile.

Since then, I have written many books, not just about Wyn, but about bear shifters, kelpies, Mars colonists and even a cult. I don't like to stick to one genre and style, there are far too many stories to tell for that. The Daughter of Winter series is currently being made into audio books and it might even be translated into German soon.

Last month, I became a full-time author. I moved to the sea and now have an office with the most amazing view. Above my desk, I have a whiteboard where I track my current projects, but there's also a Winter Princess magnet on there, always reminding me how it all started.

And now, one year after it all started, I finished my first ever series, with both a laughing and a crying eye. It's been quite the journey and it's strange to say goodbye to Wyn and her guys. I won't fully leave their world though, there are a few books planned that will be loosely connected through their setting and side characters. Ada, for example, is getting her own book, and so is Pippa, Thor's adopted daughter.

Why am I writing all this? To say thank you. I never thought I'd ever get to this point. Being a full-time author was something big and important people managed to do, but not nobodies like me.

Well, now I'm here and while it still doesn't quite feel real, I am incredibly thankful to everyone who's joined me on my journey.

You, the readers, who bought my books and motivated me to write more.

The Flock, three amazing authors who have become my best friends, co-authors and so much more.

My beta readers and my street team who make sure every book is as good as it can be. Sorry for not always giving you as much time as I would like to.

My PA, Rachel, who keeps me down to earth (I promise I'll try to do less micromanaging in the future!).

My friends, online and offline, who've put up with my craziness for years.

My fellow authors, who have let me into their community and taught me so much.

And of course my family, who turned me into a bookworm and always make sure that I stay realistic in my ambitions and plans ;)

Now I better stop before tears ruin my keyboard. To many more magical journeys into my imagination!

Skye MacKinnon

Summer 2018

About the Author

Skye MacKinnon is a USA Today & International Bestselling Author whose books are filled with strong heroines who don't have to choose.

She embraces her Scottishness with fantastical Scottish settings and a dash of mythology, no matter if she's writing about Celtic gods, cat shifters, or the streets of Edinburgh.

When she's not typing away at her favourite cafe, Skye loves dried mango, as much exotic tea as she can squeeze into her cupboards, and being covered in pet hair by her tiny demonic cat.

Subscribe to her newsletter:
skyemackinnon.com/newsletter

facebook.com/skyemackinnonauthor

twitter.com/skye_mackinnon

instagram.com/skyemackinnonauthor

bookbub.com/authors/skye-mackinnon

goodreads.com/SkyeMacKinnon

Also By

Find all of Skye's books on her website, skyemackinnon.com, where you can also order signed paperbacks. Many of her books are also available as audiobooks.

Claiming Her Bears (Post-apocalyptic bear shifter RH)

Rescued by Bears

Protected by Bears

Craved by Bears

>> Box set

Infernal Descent (paranormal RH based on Dante's Inferno, co-written with Bea Paige)

Hell's Calling

Hell's Weeping

Hell's Burning

>> Box set

Seven Wardens (Paranormal RH co-written with Laura Greenwood)

From the Deeps

Into the Mists

Beneath the Earth

Within the Flames

Above the Waves

Under the Ice

Rule the Dark

Prequel: Beyond the Loch

Spin-off: Through the Storms

>> Box set (books 1-4)

>> Box set (books 5-7)

The Lost Siren (post-apocalyptic, paranormal RH co-written with Liza Street)

Song of Blood

Lullaby of Death

Melody of Souls

Starlight Highlanders Mail Order Brides (m/f alien romance, part of the Intergalactic Dating Agency)

Thorrn

Eron

Cyle

Between Rebels (sci-fi RH set in the Planet Athion shared world)

Stolen By Them

Guarded By Them

Chosen By Them

>> Box Set

The Intergalactic Guide to Humans (sci-fi romance, RH, m/f and fmf)

Alien Abduction for Beginners

Alien Abduction for Professionals

Alien Abduction for Experts

Alien Abduction for Pirates

Alien Abduction for Santa

The Mars Diaries (Sci-fi RH linked to the Claiming Her Bears series)

Alone

Hidden

Found

>> Box Set

Through the Gates (dystopian RH co-written with Rebecca Royce)

Purgatory City

Defiance (contemporary dark RH)

Frozen Heart

Loving Heart

Broken Spirit

Stolen Soul

Academy of Time (time travel academy standalones)

Taking Her Vikings

Exploring Her Professor

Saving His Queen

Catnip Assassins (urban fantasy reverse harem)

Meow

Scratch

Purrr

Hisss

Lick

Claw

Roar

Thud (Christmas special)

>> Box set Books 1-4

>> Box set Books 5-7

>> Box set Books 1-7

Aliens and Animals (sci-fi romance co-written with Arizona Tape)

The Alien's Zookeeper

The Alien's Veterinarian

Daughter of Winter Series (Paranormal reverse harem)

Winter Princess

Winter Heiress

Winter Queen

Winter Goddess

>> Box set

Mother of Gods (prequel)

Demon's Revenge (spin-off)